ST
-and-
SCONES
in
THE STICKY WAND

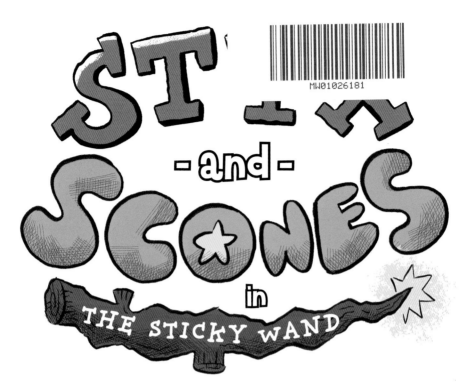

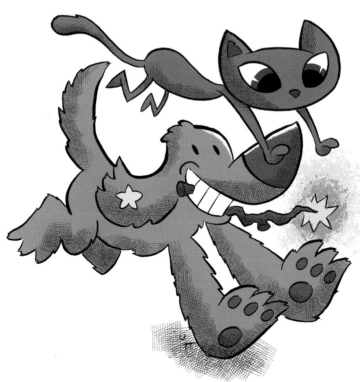

For Mom Mom Willis

SIMON SPOTLIGHT
An imprint of Simon & Schuster Children's Publishing Division
1230 Avenue of the Americas, New York, New York 10020
This Simon Spotlight edition June 2023
Copyright © 2023 by Jay Cooper
All rights reserved, including the right of reproduction in whole or in
part in any form. SIMON SPOTLIGHT, READY-TO-READ, and colophon
are registered trademarks of Simon & Schuster, Inc.
For information about special discounts for bulk purchases, please contact
Simon & Schuster Special Sales at 1-866-506-1949 or business@simonandschuster.com.
The Simon & Schuster Speakers Bureau can bring authors to your live event. For more information
or to book an event contact the Simon & Schuster Speakers Bureau
at 1-866-248-3049 or visit our website at www.simonspeakers.com.
Manufactured in China 0223 SCP
2 4 6 8 10 9 7 5 3 1
This book has been cataloged with the Library of Congress.
ISBN 978-1-6659-3537-1 (hc) • ISBN 978-1-6659-3536-4 (pbk)
ISBN 978-1-6659-3538-8 (ebook)

STYX and SCONES in THE STICKY WAND

written and illustrated by
Jay Cooper

Ready-to-Read *GRAPHICS*

Simon Spotlight
New York London Toronto Sydney New Delhi

HOW TO READ THIS BOOK

Styx is here to give you some helpful tips on reading this book.

If there is a box like this one, read the words inside the box first. Then read the words in the speech or thought bubbles below it...

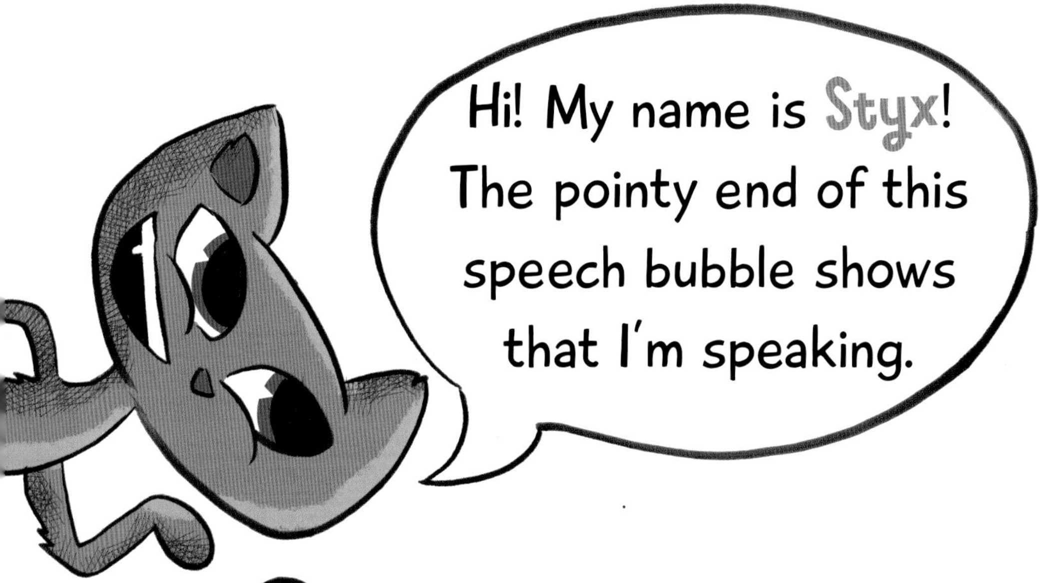
Hi! My name is Styx! The pointy end of this speech bubble shows that I'm speaking.

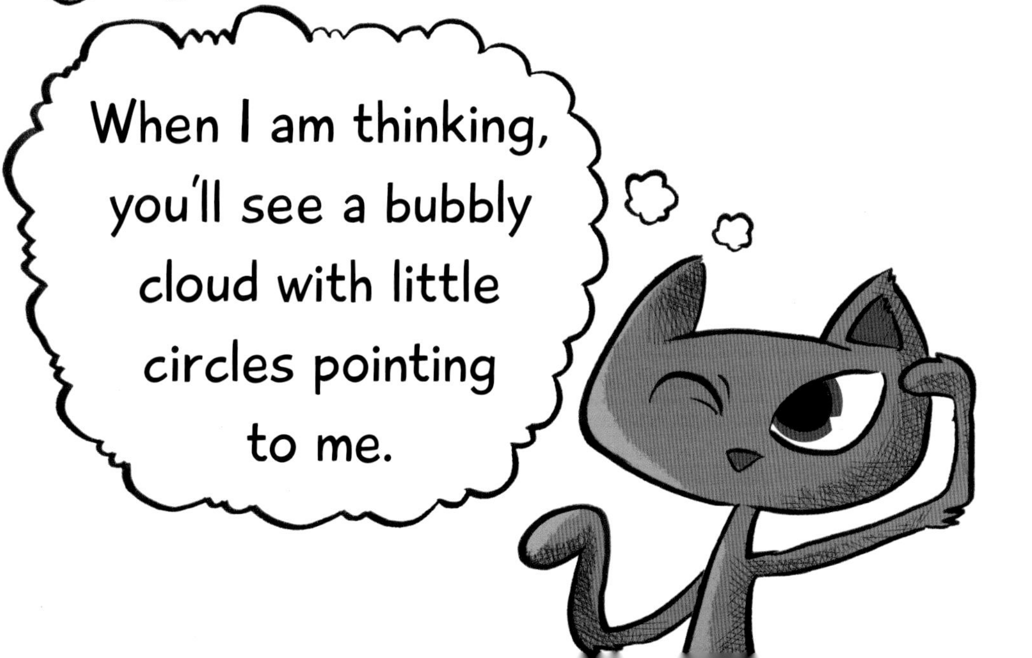
When I am thinking, you'll see a bubbly cloud with little circles pointing to me.

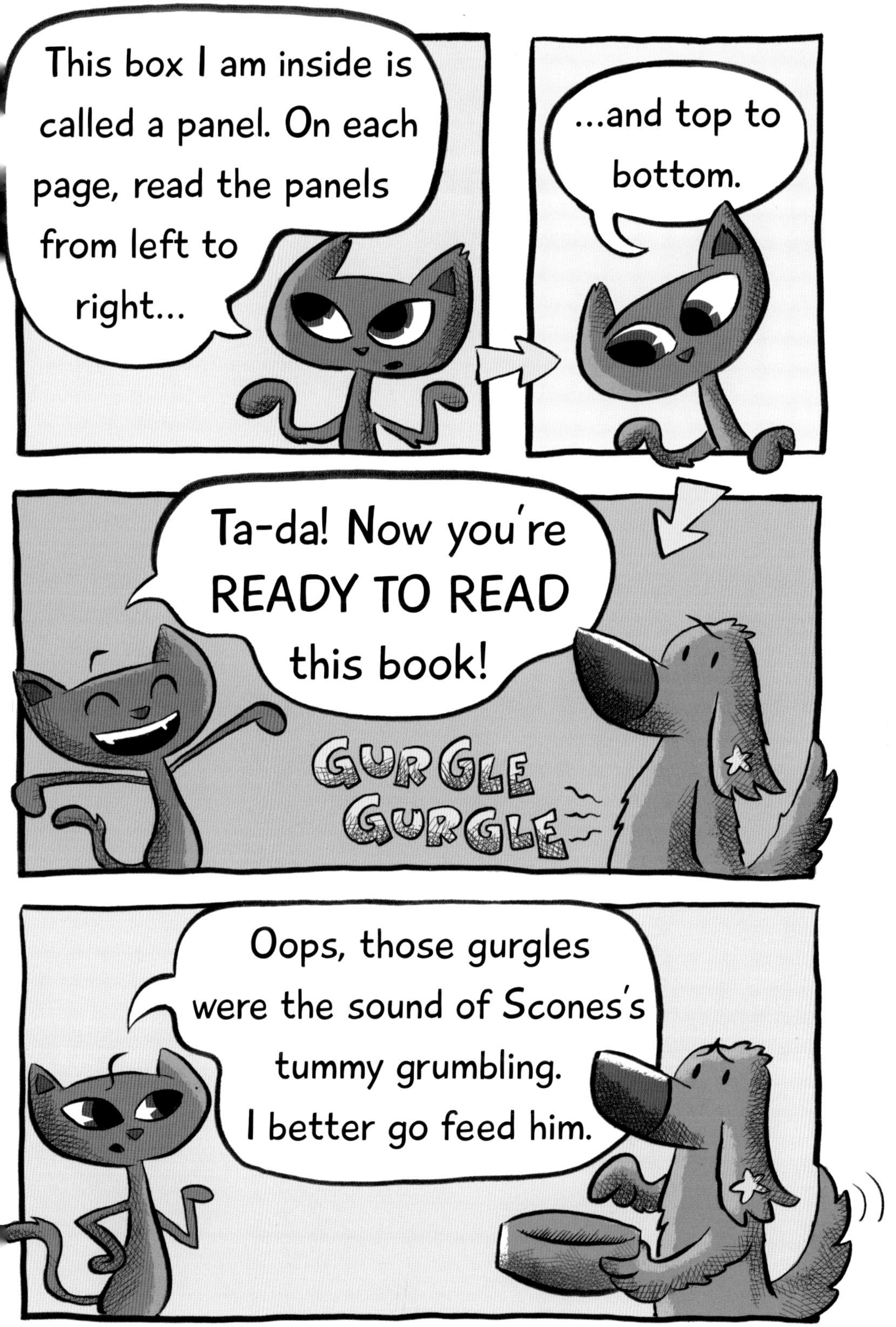
This box I am inside is called a panel. On each page, read the panels from left to right...
...and top to bottom.
Ta-da! Now you're READY TO READ this book!
GURGLE GURGLE
Oops, those gurgles were the sound of Scones's tummy grumbling. I better go feed him.

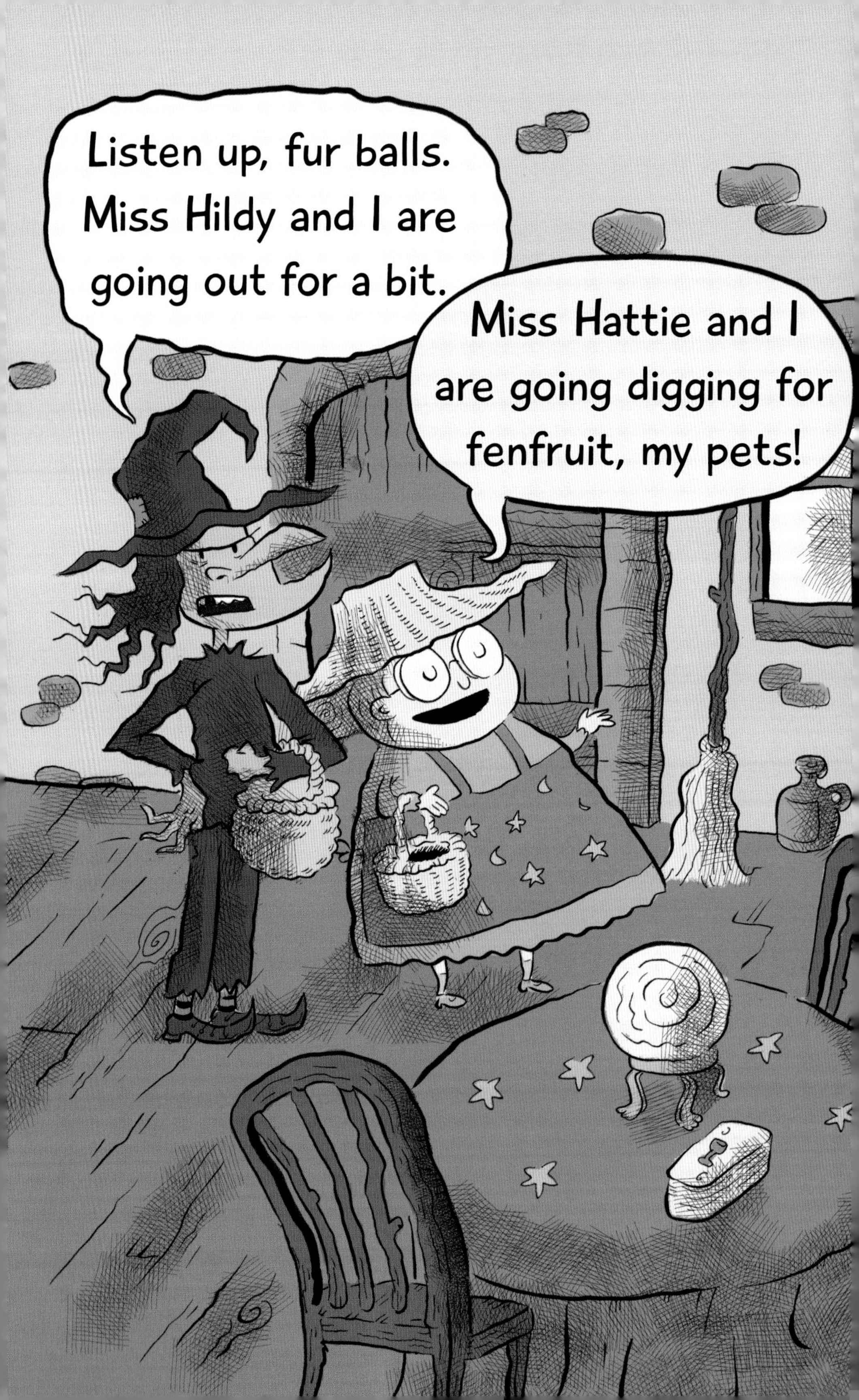
Listen up, fur balls. Miss Hildy and I are going out for a bit.
Miss Hattie and I are going digging for fenfruit, my pets!

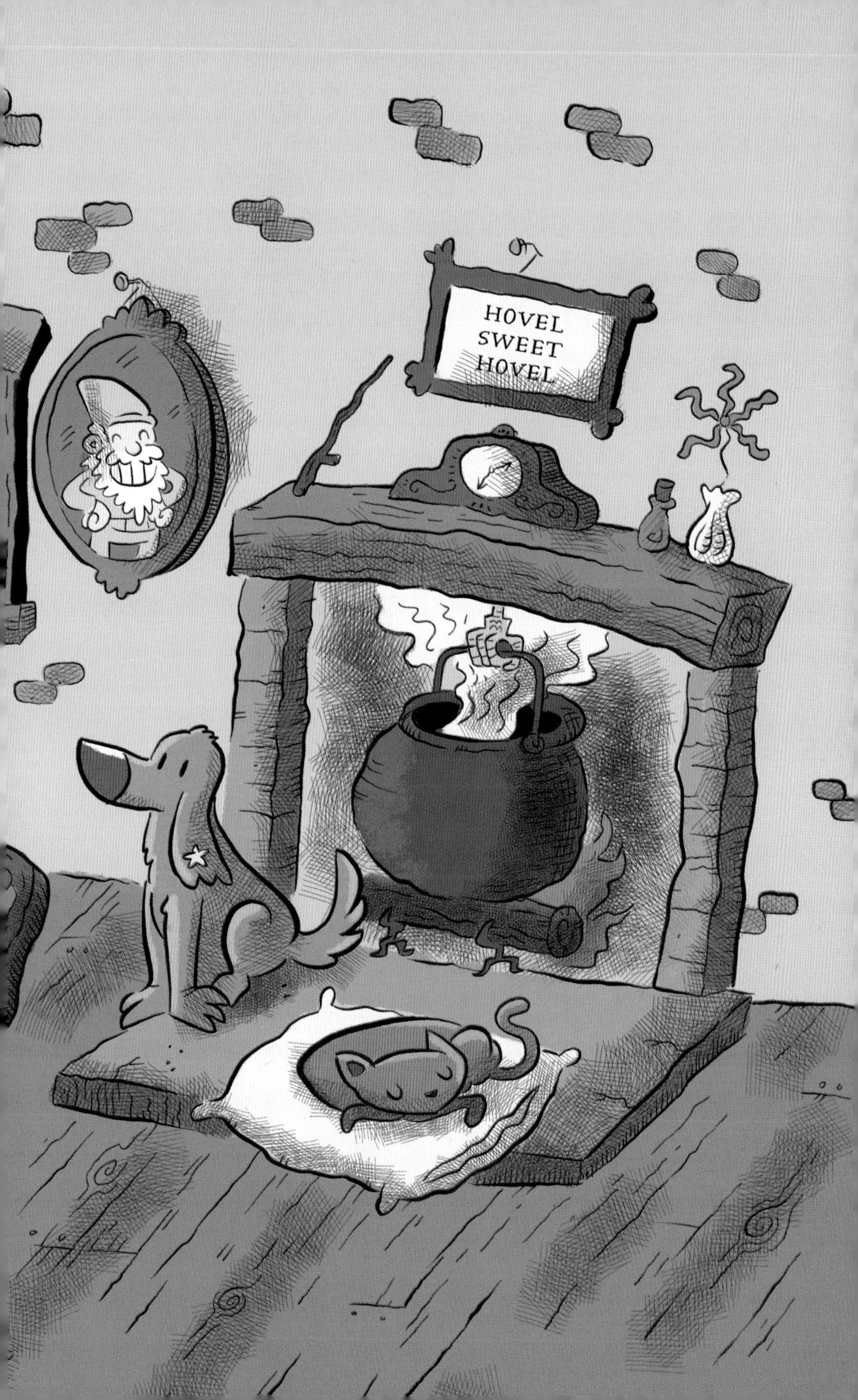
HOVEL
SWEET
HOVEL

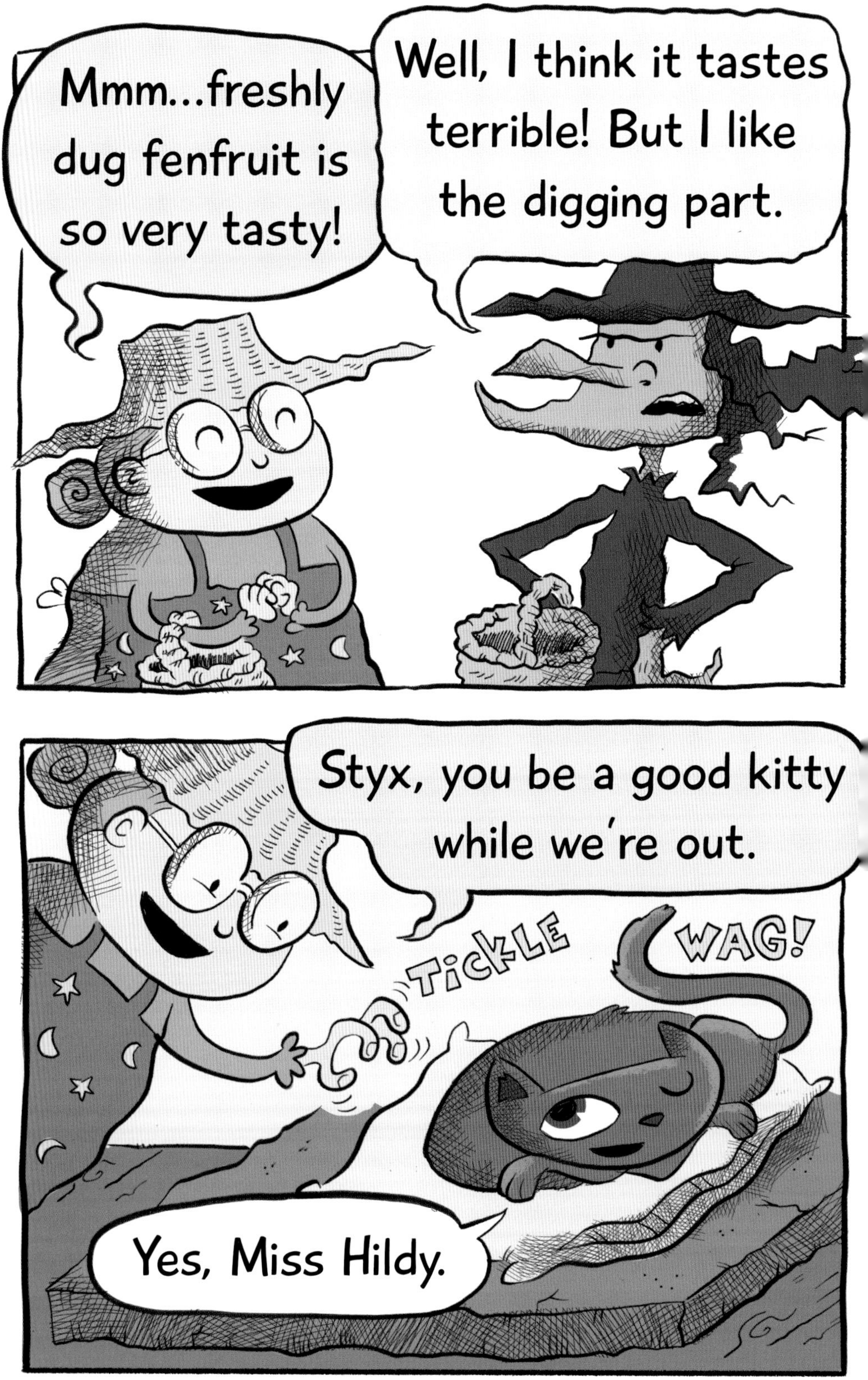
Mmm...freshly dug fenfruit is so very tasty!
Well, I think it tastes terrible! But I like the digging part.
Styx, you be a good kitty while we're out.
TICKLE
WAG!
Yes, Miss Hildy.

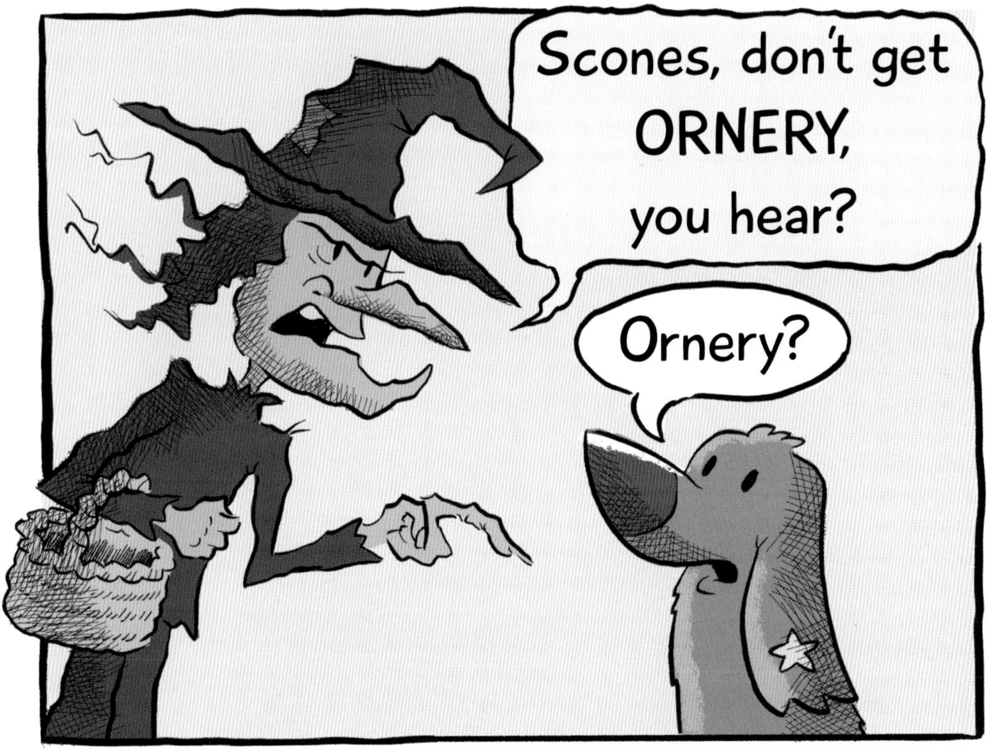
Scones, don't get ORNERY, you hear?
Ornery?

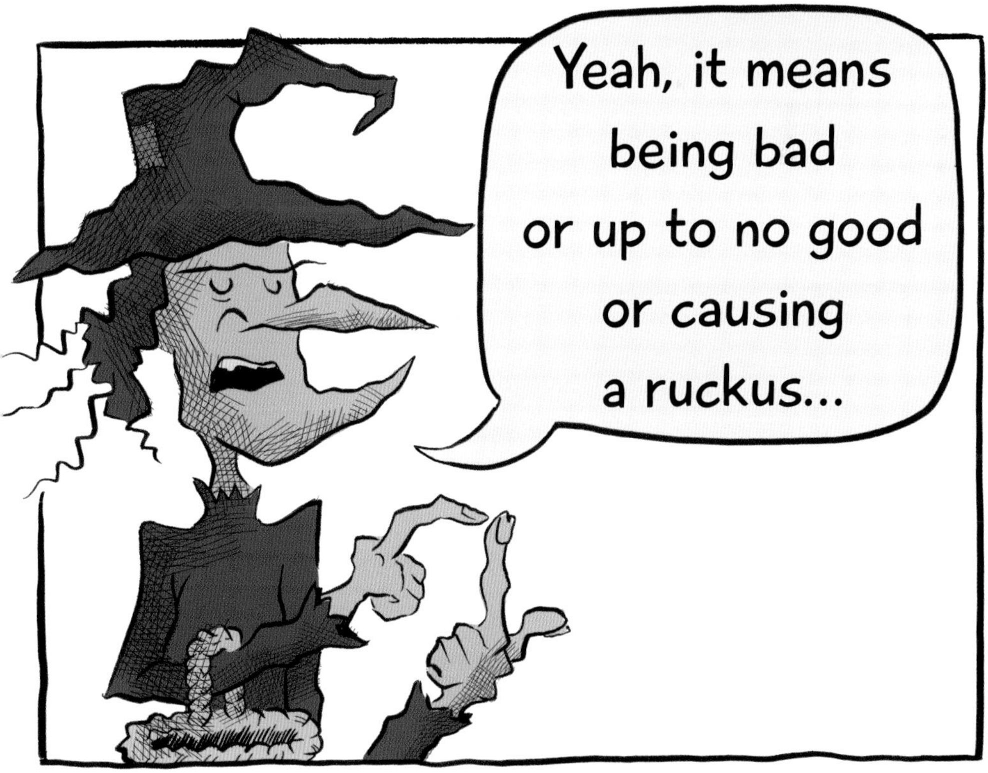
Yeah, it means being bad or up to no good or causing a ruckus...

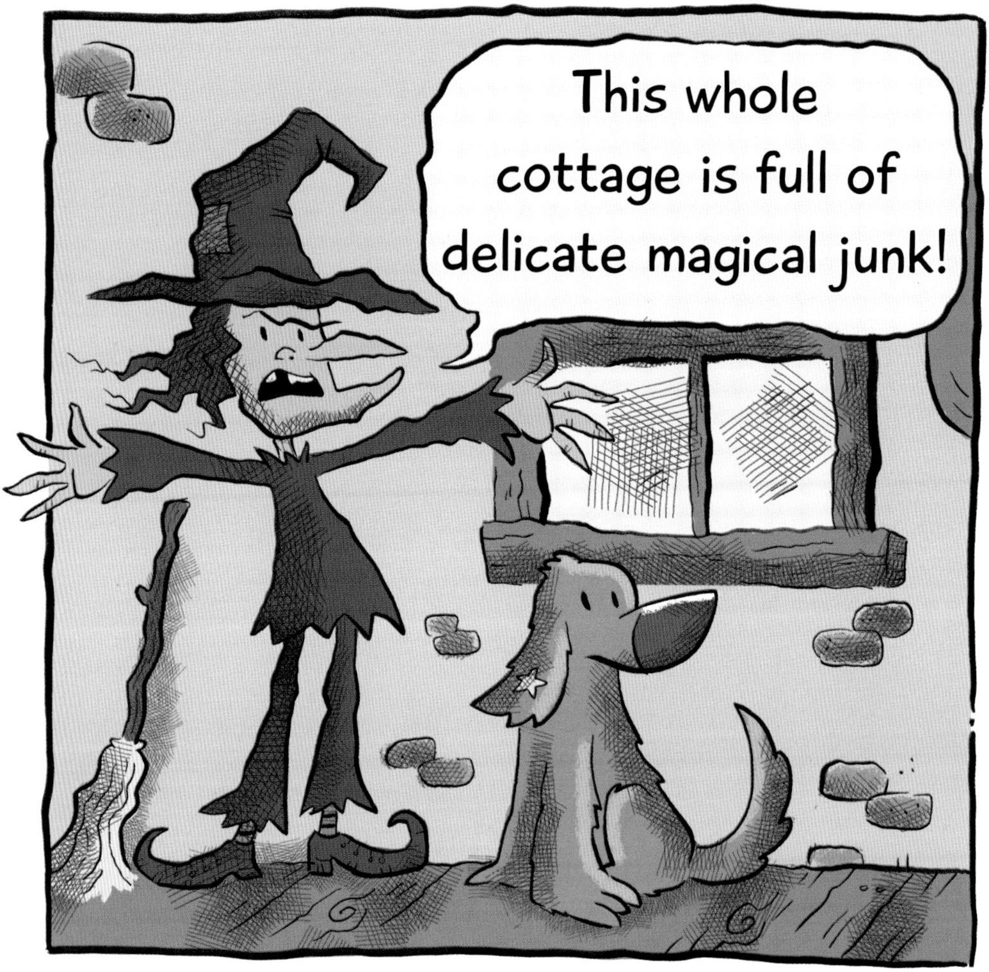
This whole cottage is full of delicate magical junk!

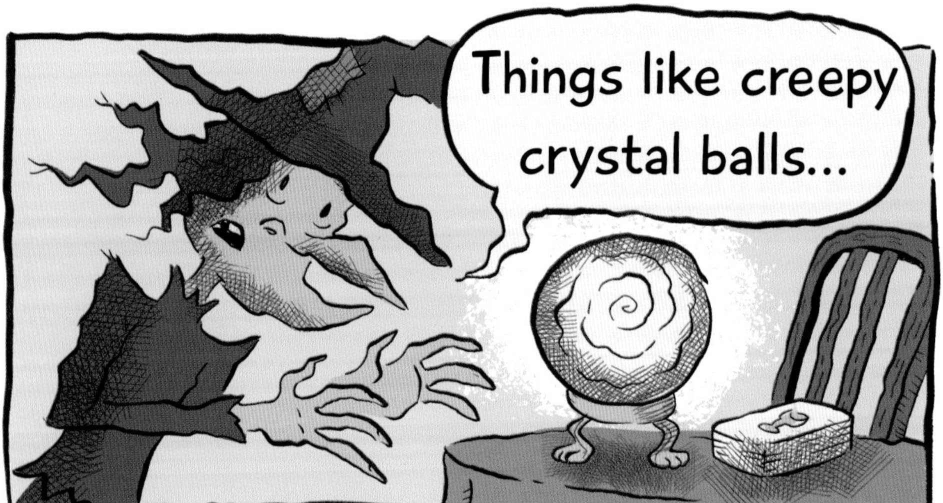
Things like creepy crystal balls...

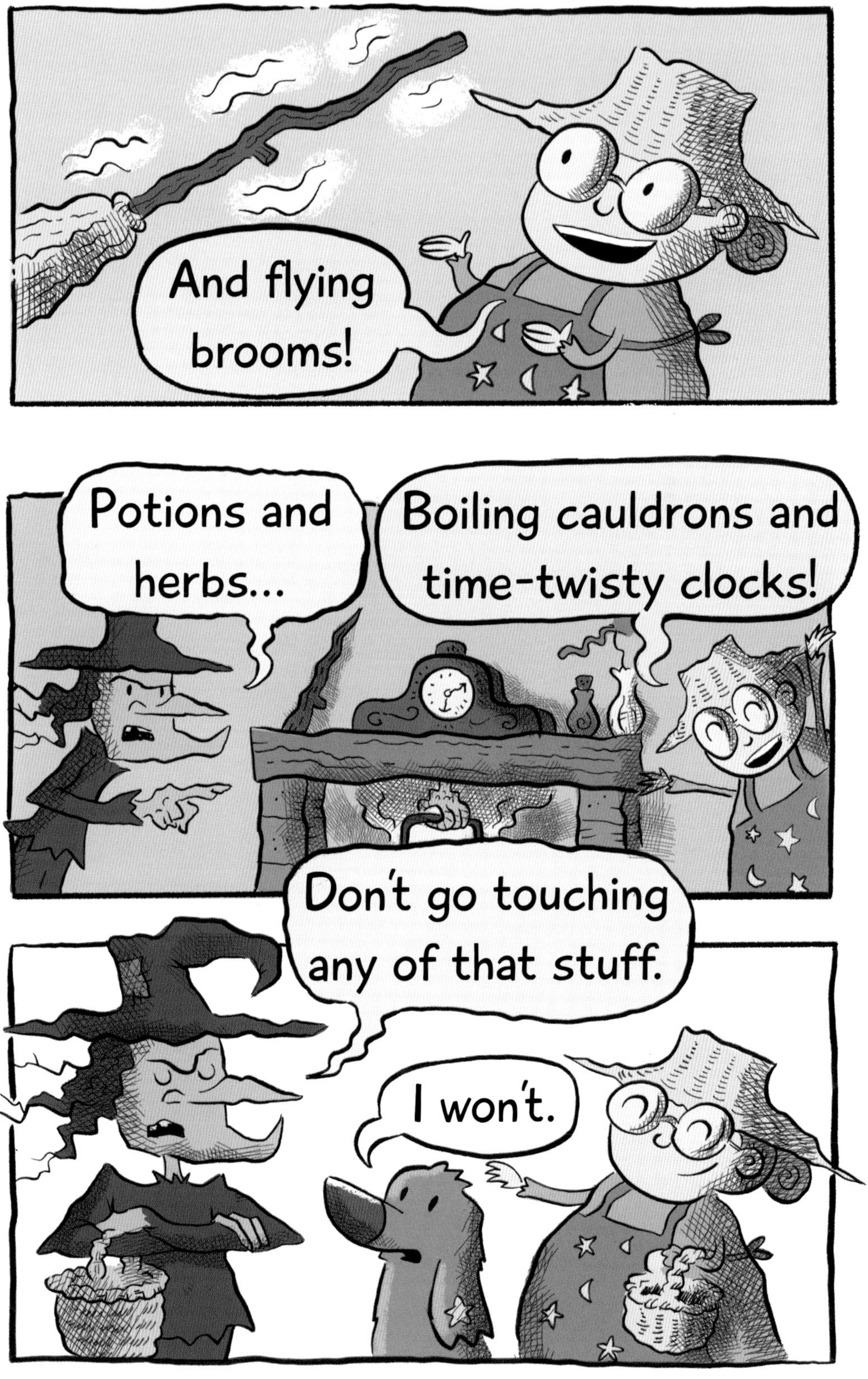
And flying brooms!
Potions and herbs...
Boiling cauldrons and time-twisty clocks!
Don't go touching any of that stuff.
I won't.

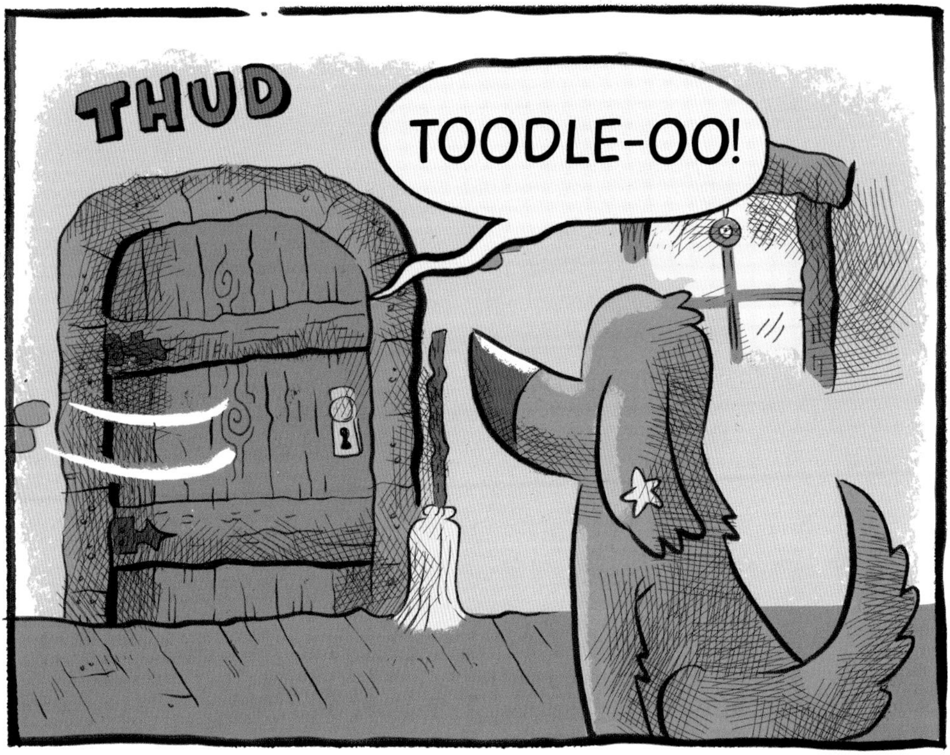
THUD
TOODLE-OO!

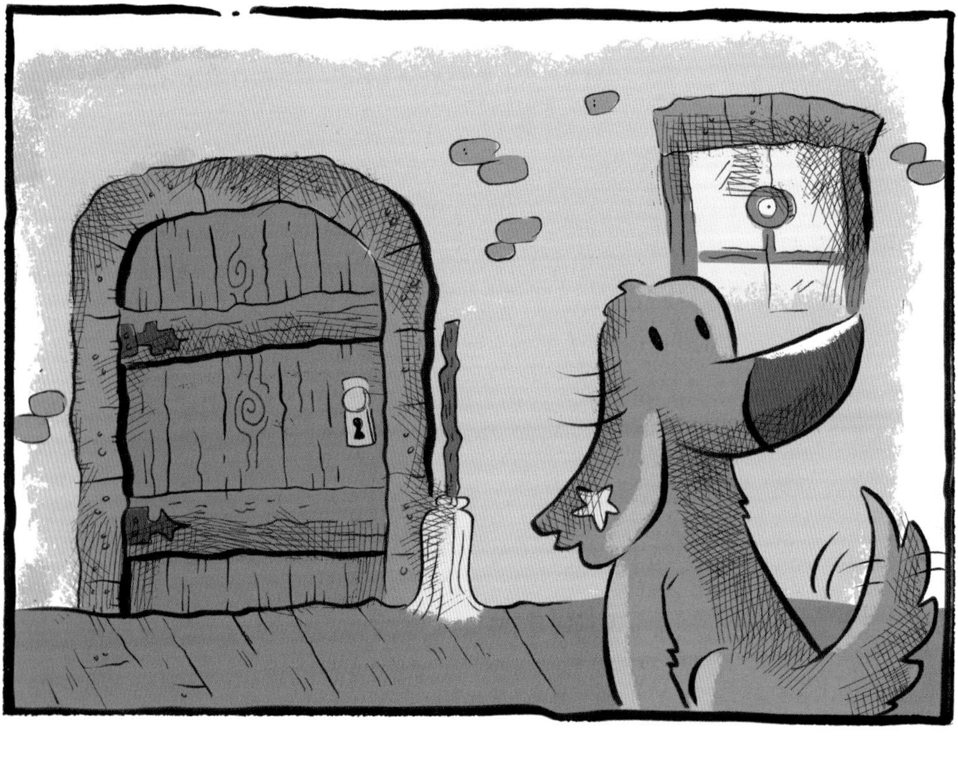

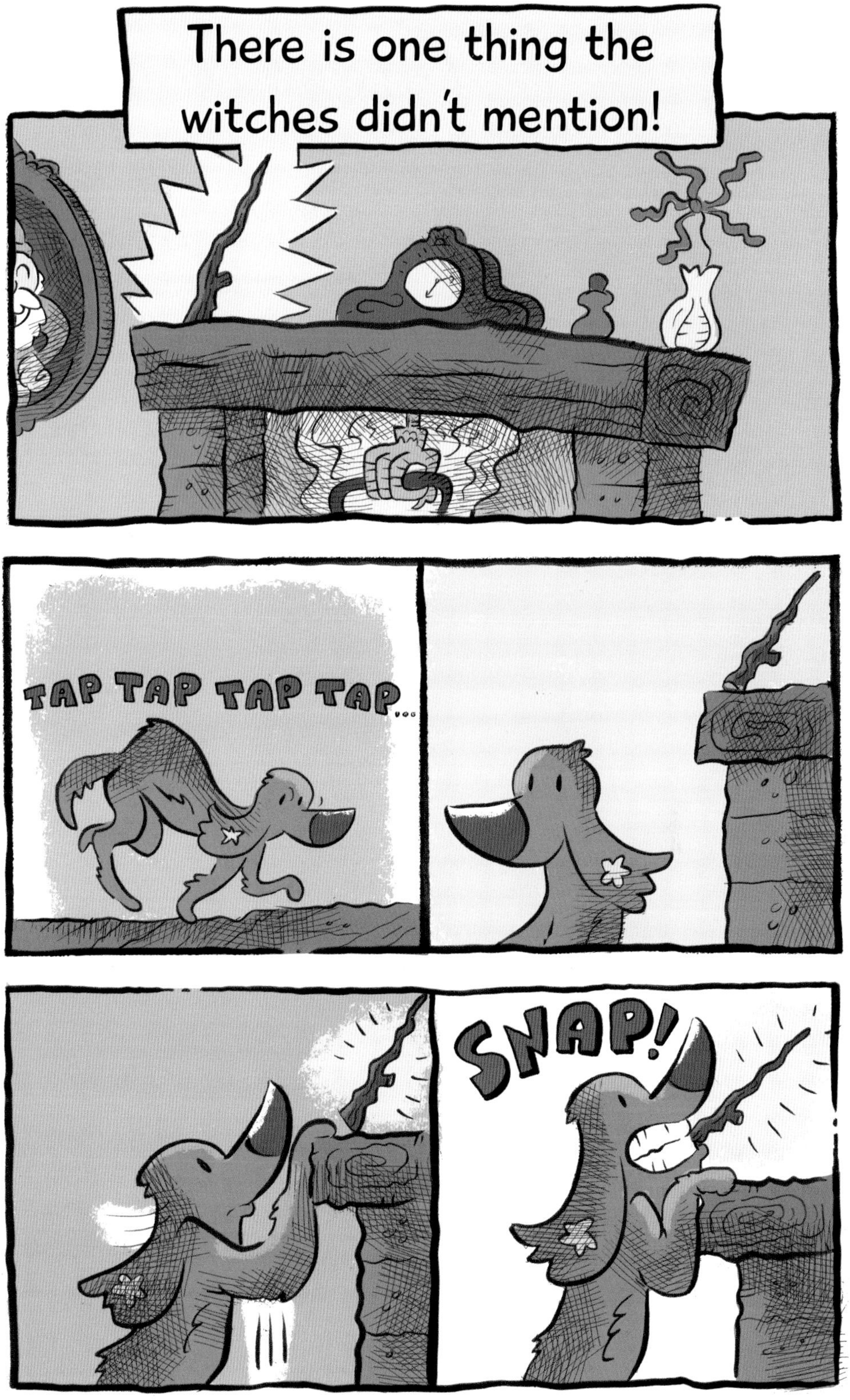
There is one thing the witches didn't mention!
TAP TAP TAP TAP...
SNAP!

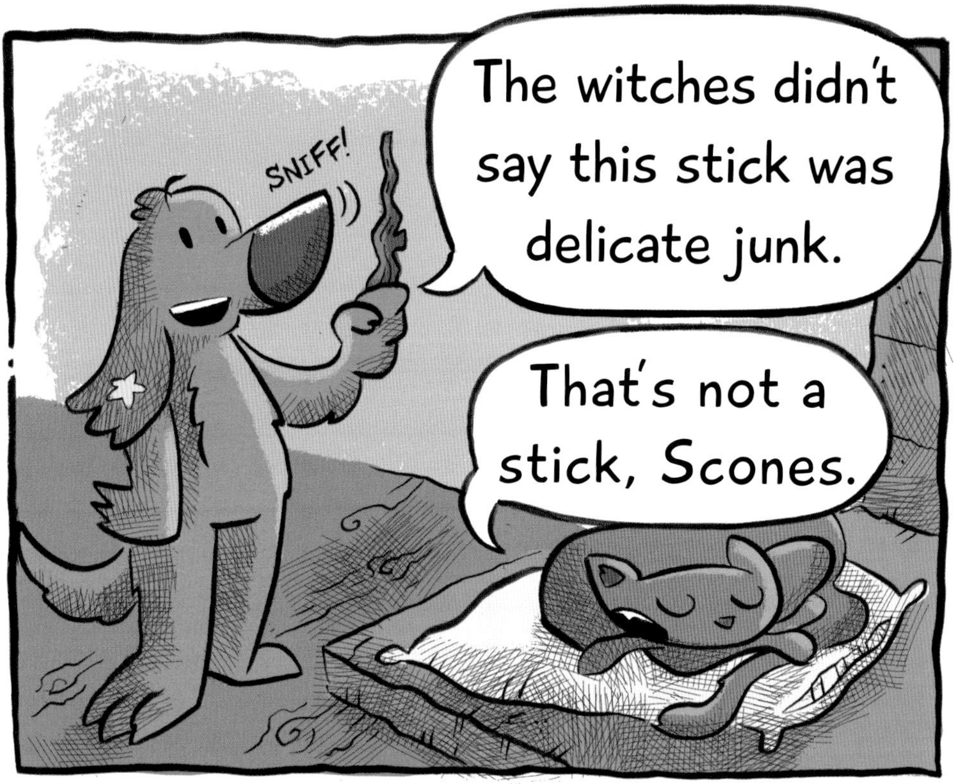
SNIFF!
The witches didn't say this stick was delicate junk.
That's not a stick, Scones.

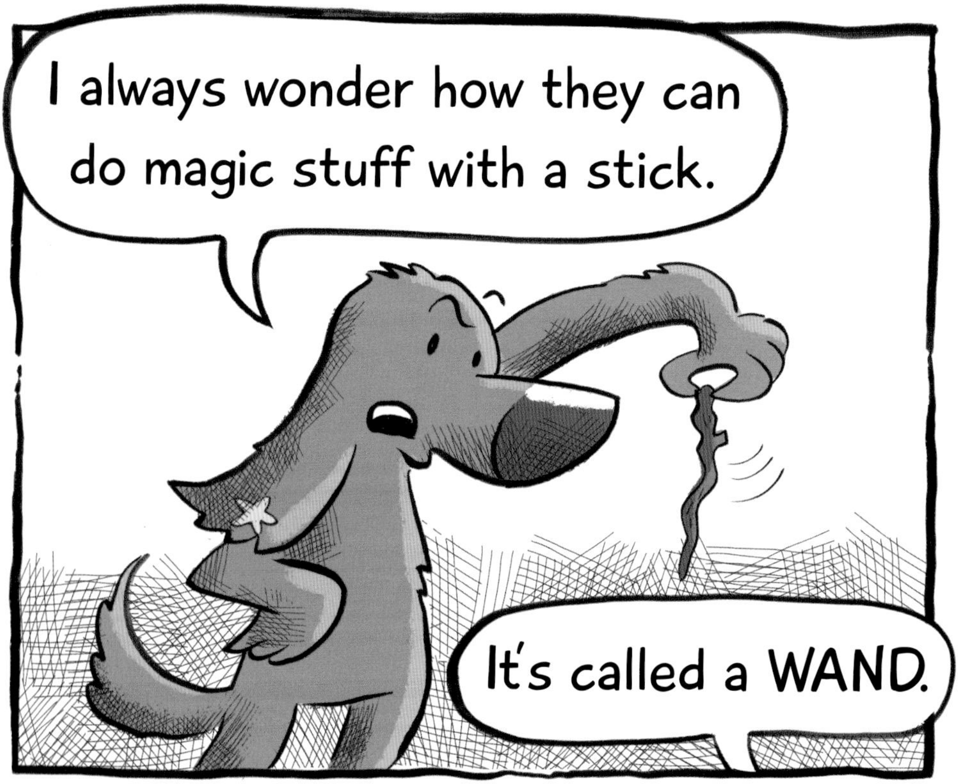
I always wonder how they can do magic stuff with a stick.
It's called a WAND.

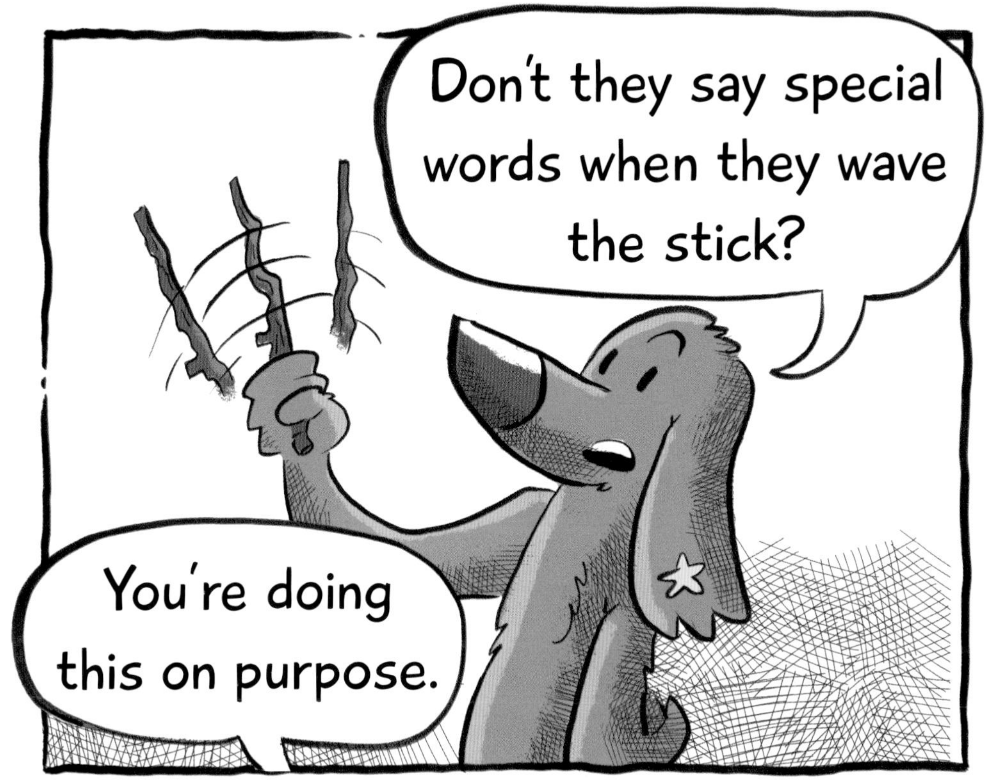
Don't they say special words when they wave the stick?
You're doing this on purpose.

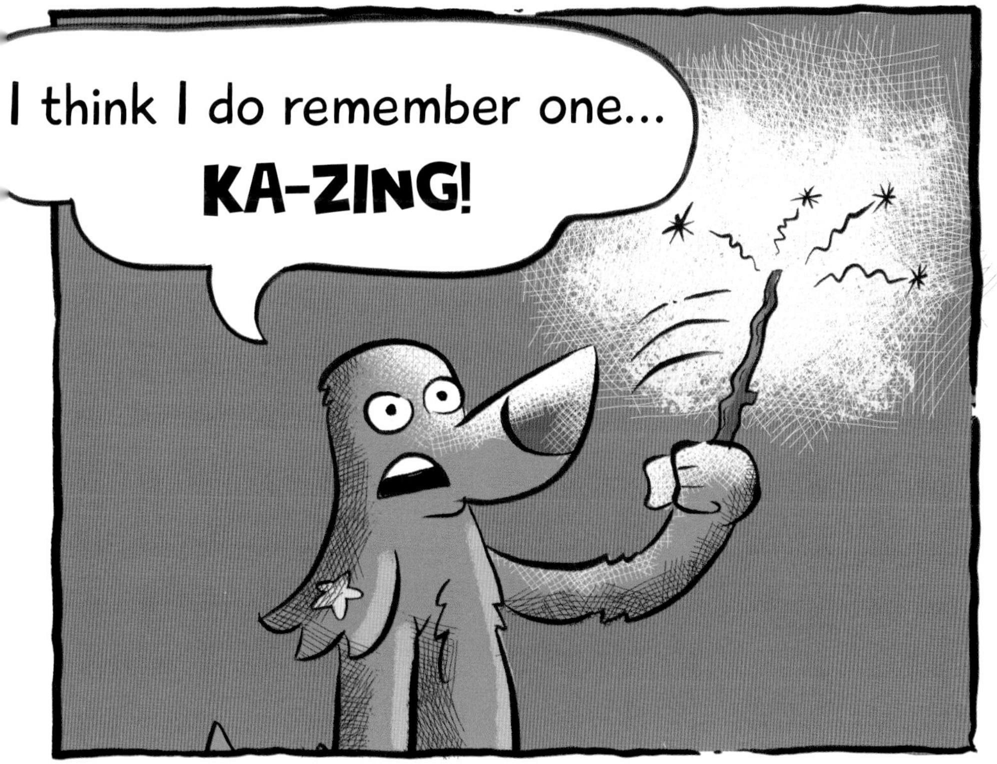
I think I do remember one...
KA-ZING!

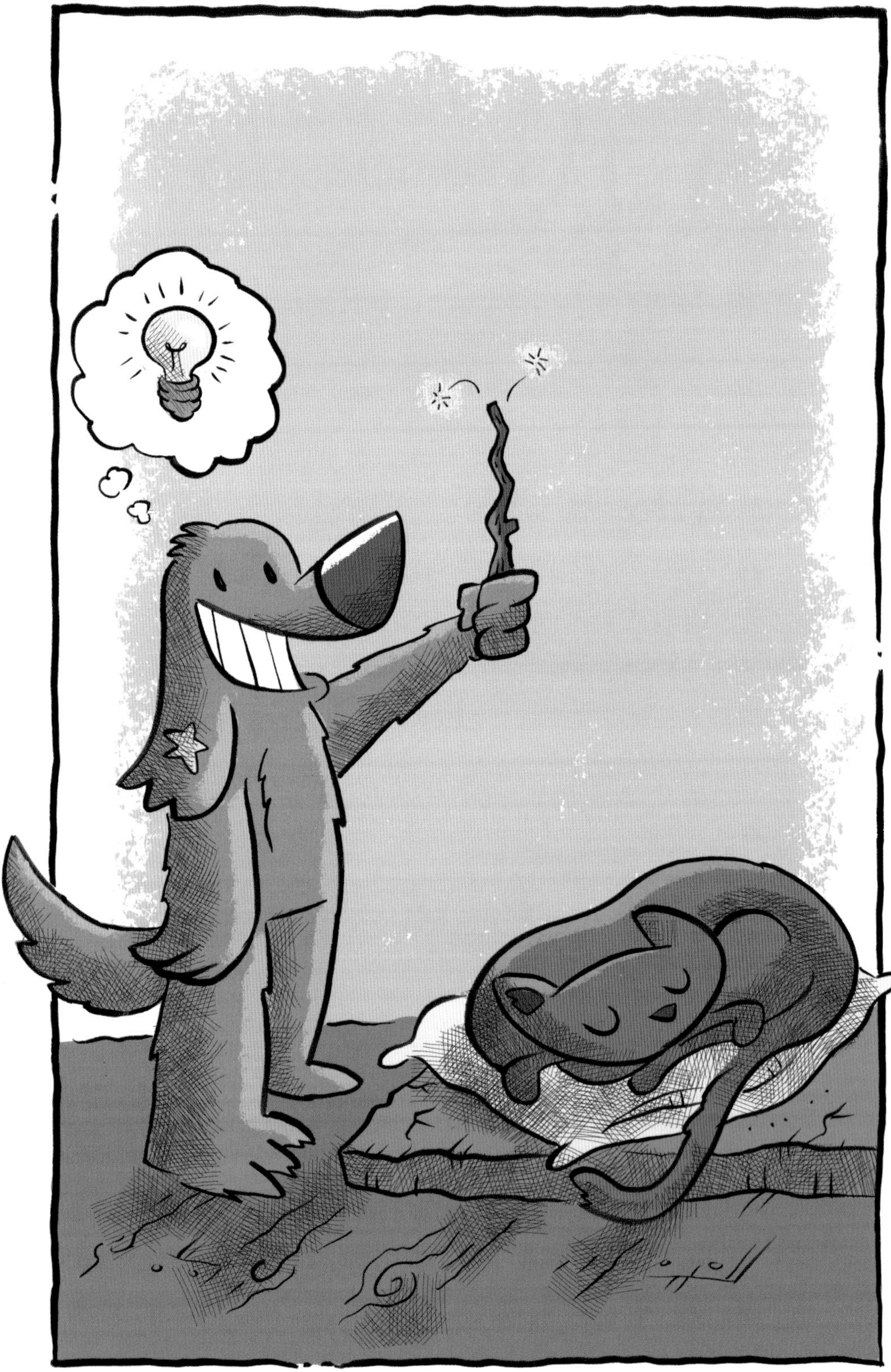

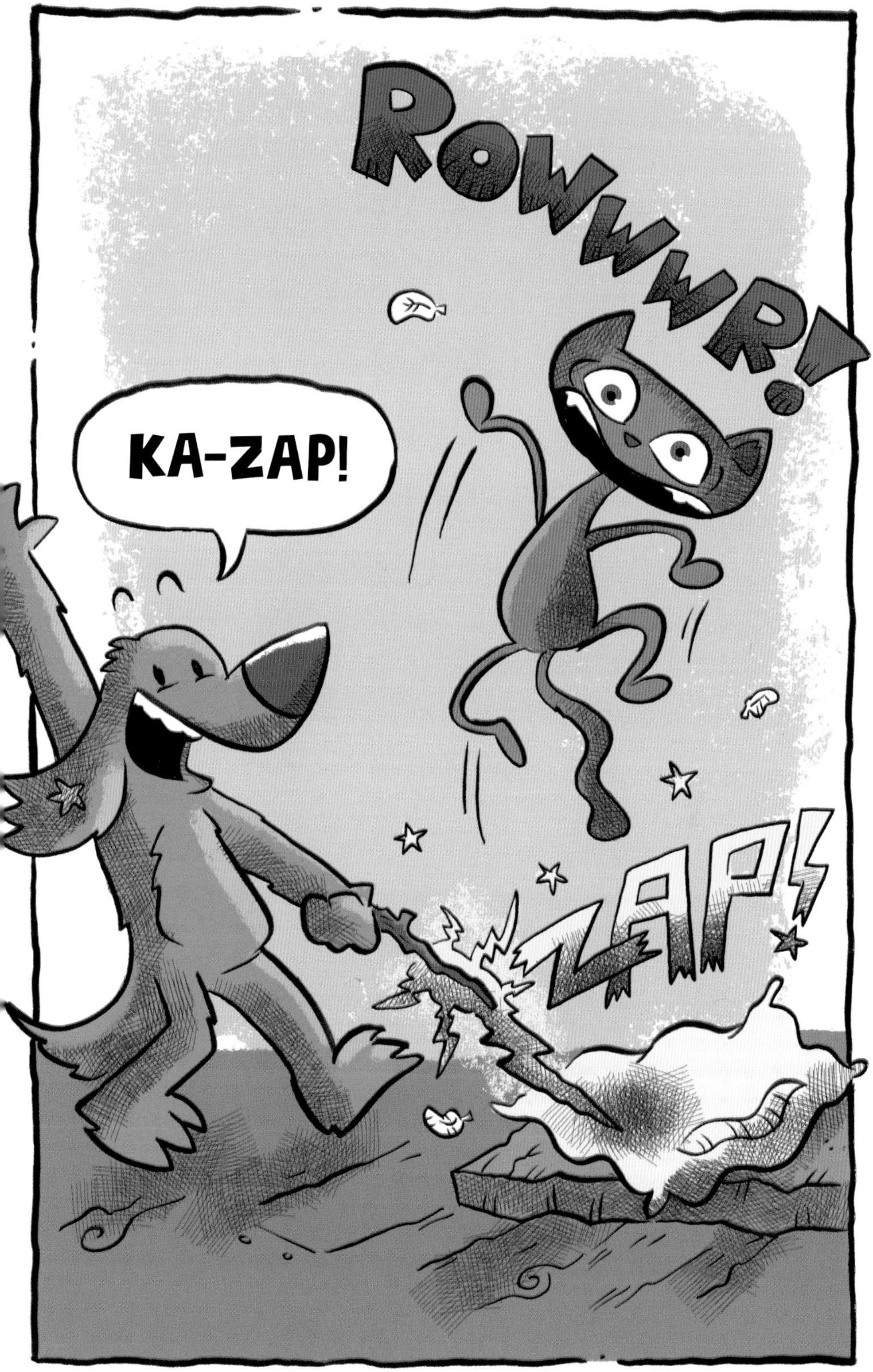
ROWWWR!
KA-ZAP!
ZAP!

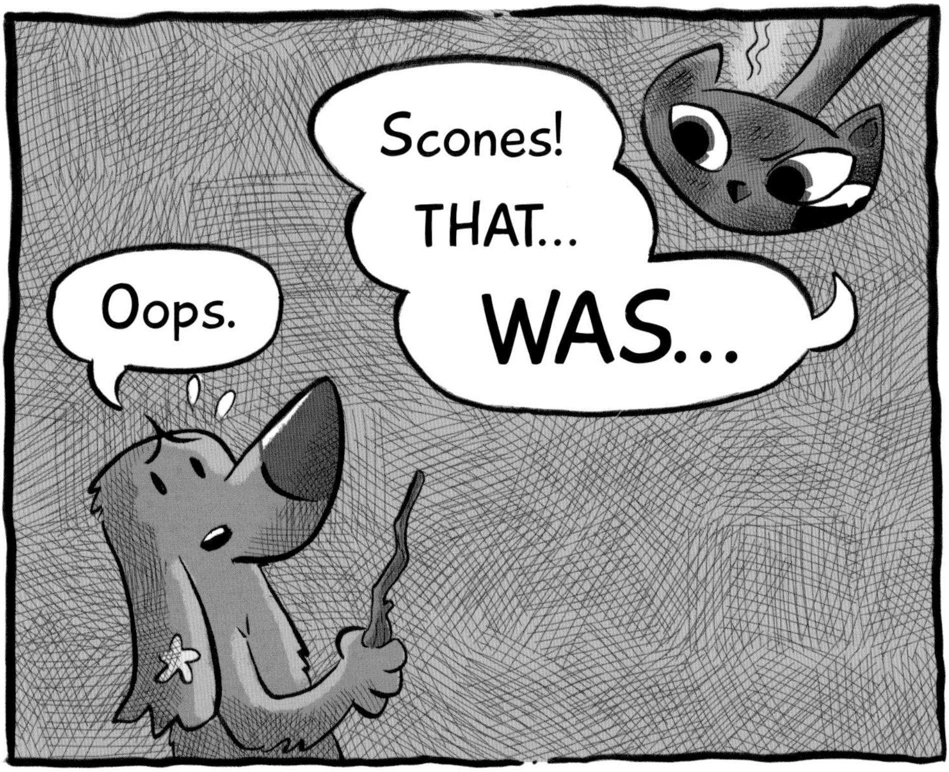
Oops.
Scones! THAT... WAS...

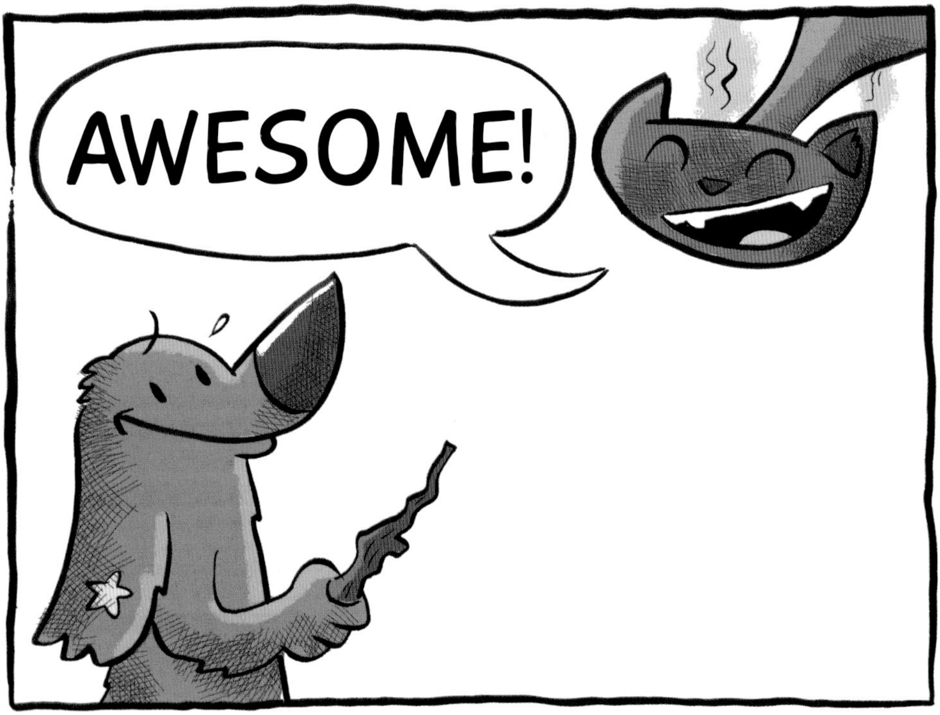
AWESOME!

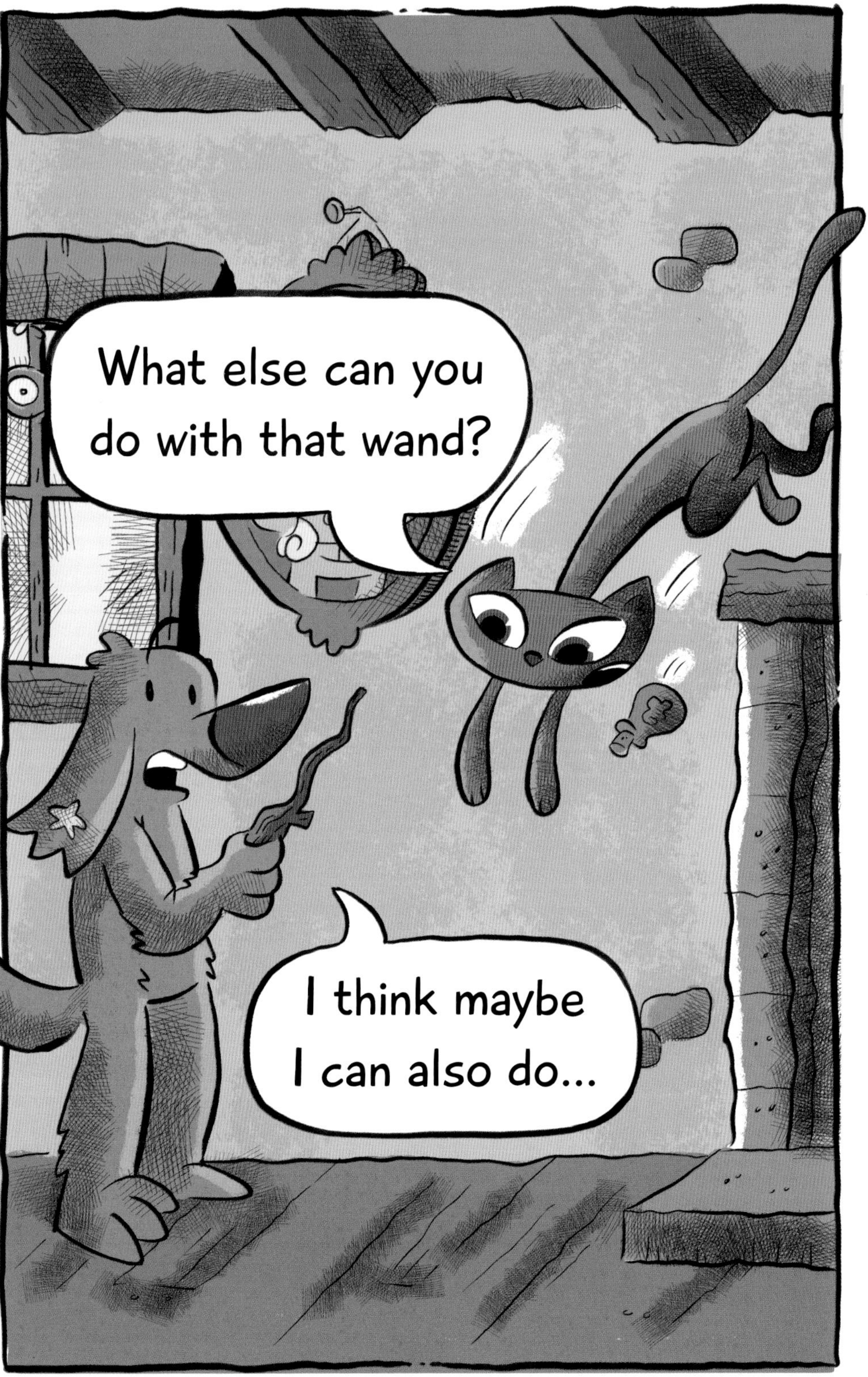
What else can you do with that wand?
I think maybe I can also do...

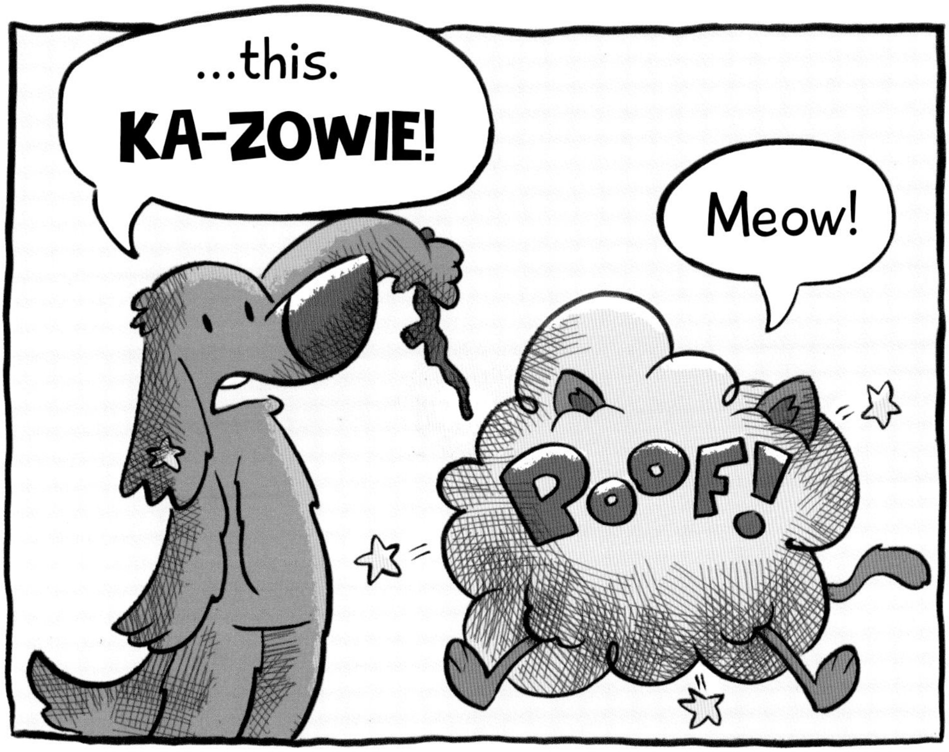
...this.
KA-ZOWIE!
Meow!
POOF!

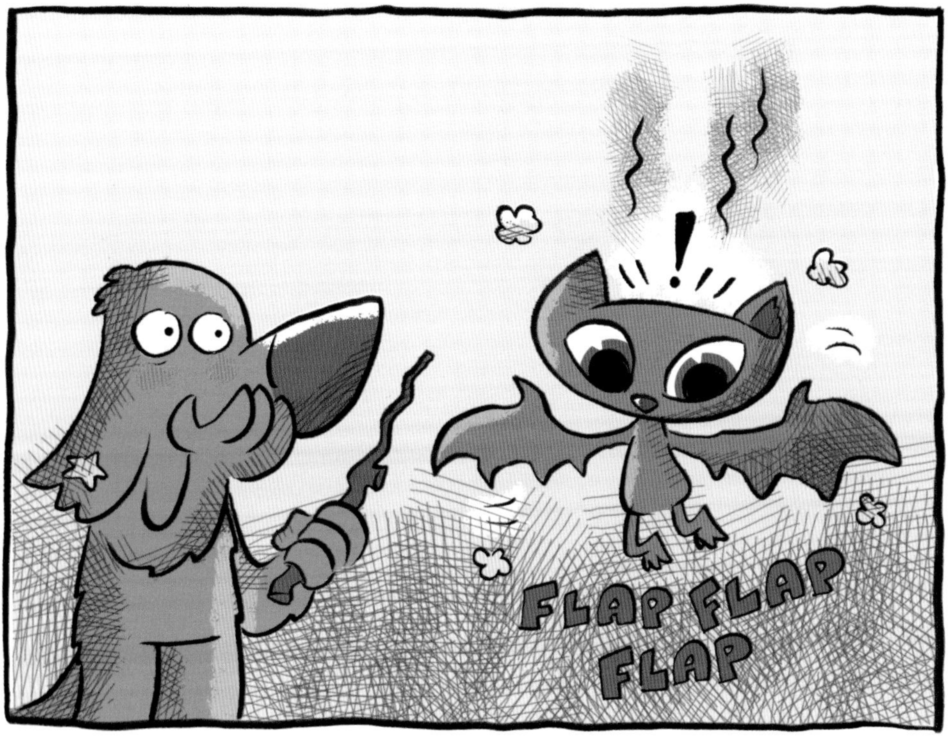
!
FLAP FLAP
FLAP

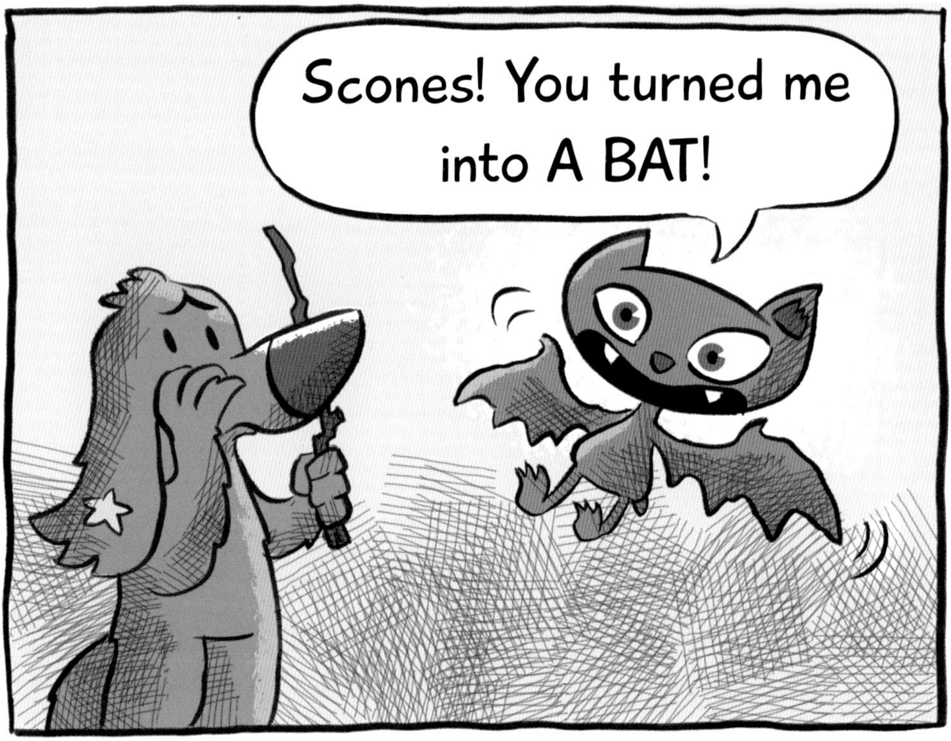
Scones! You turned me into A BAT!

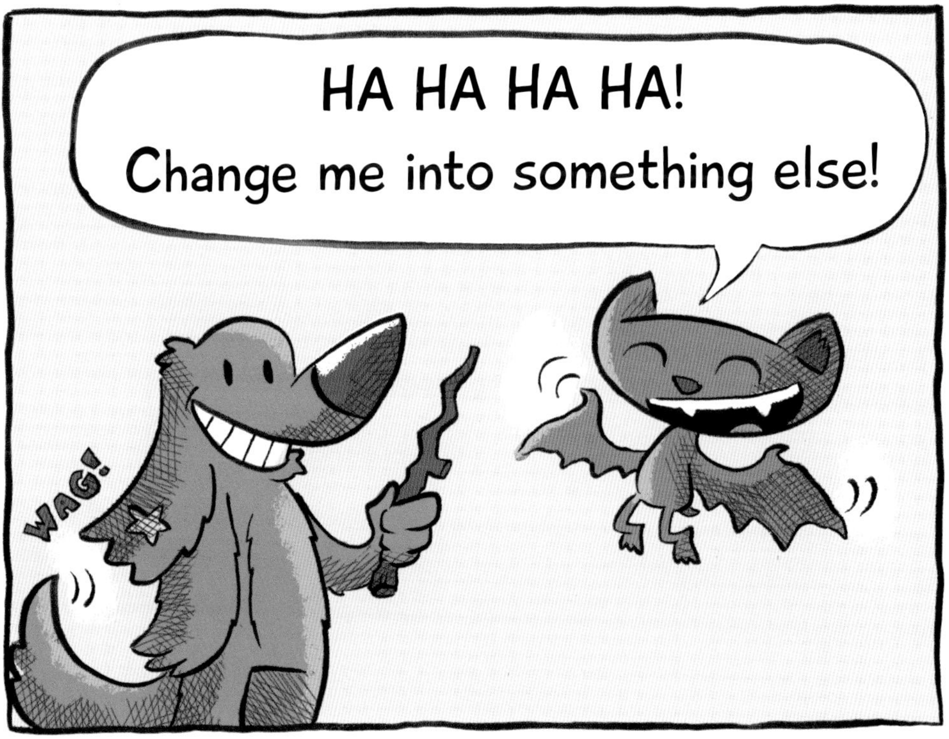
HA HA HA HA!
Change me into something else!
WAG!

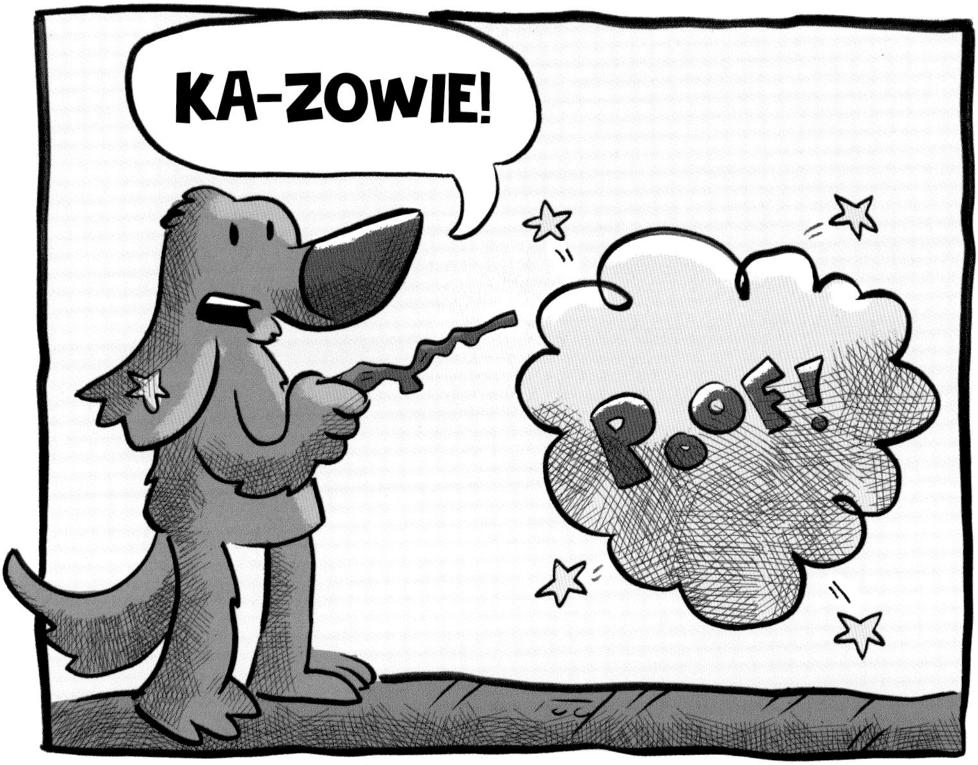
KA-ZOWIE!
POOF!

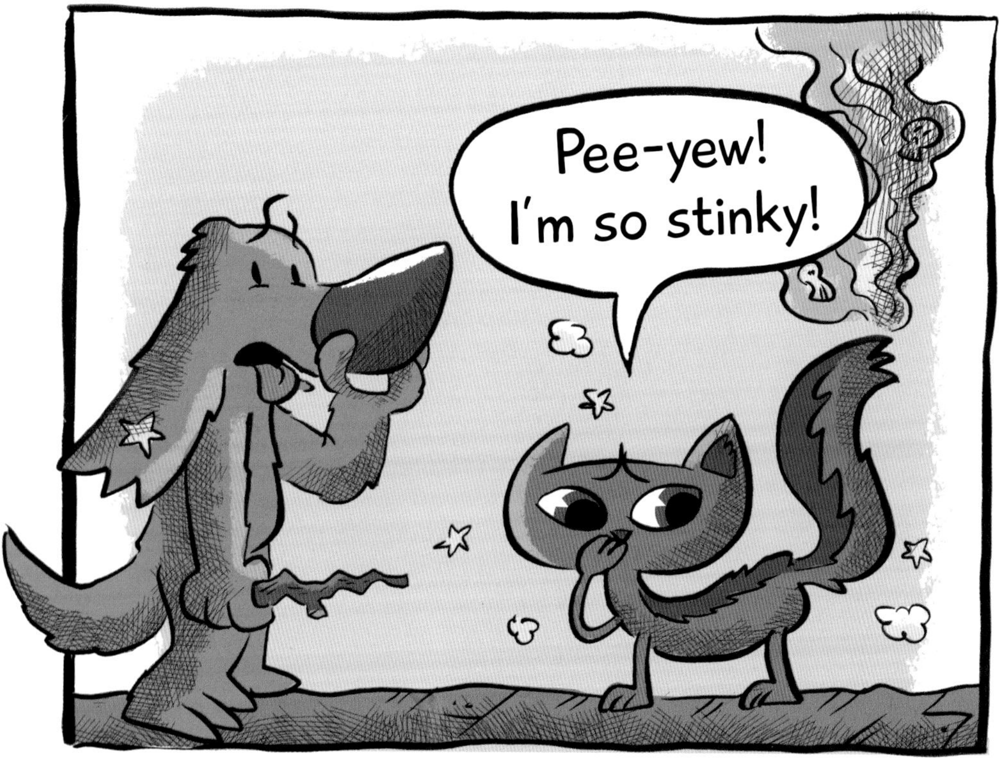
Pee-yew!
I'm so stinky!

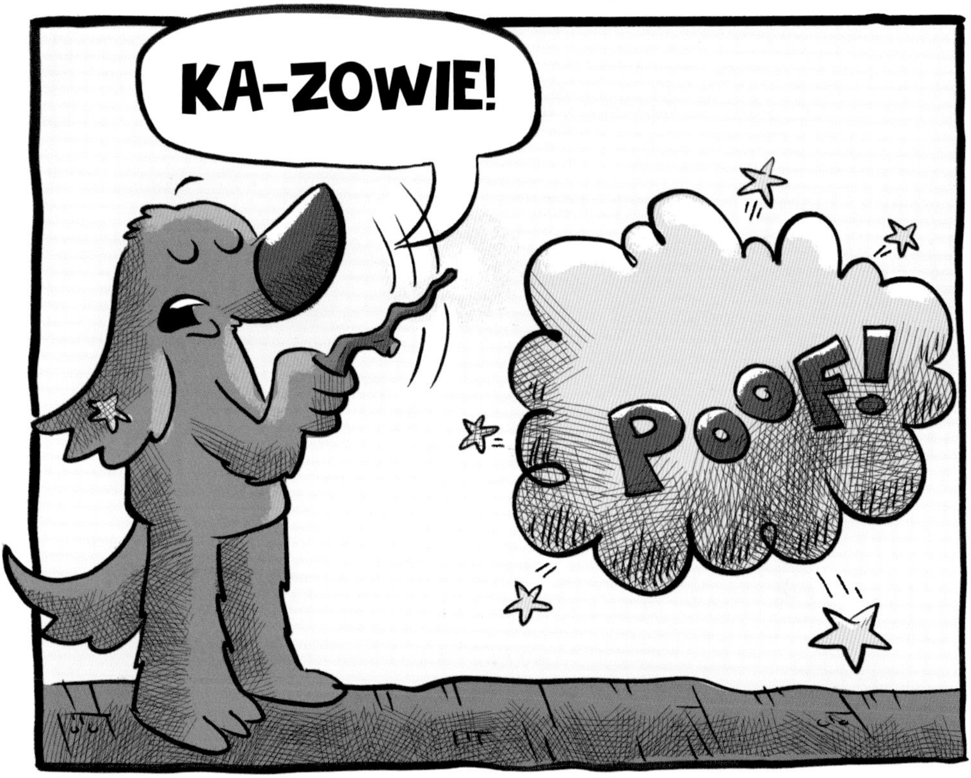
KA-ZOWIE!
POOF!

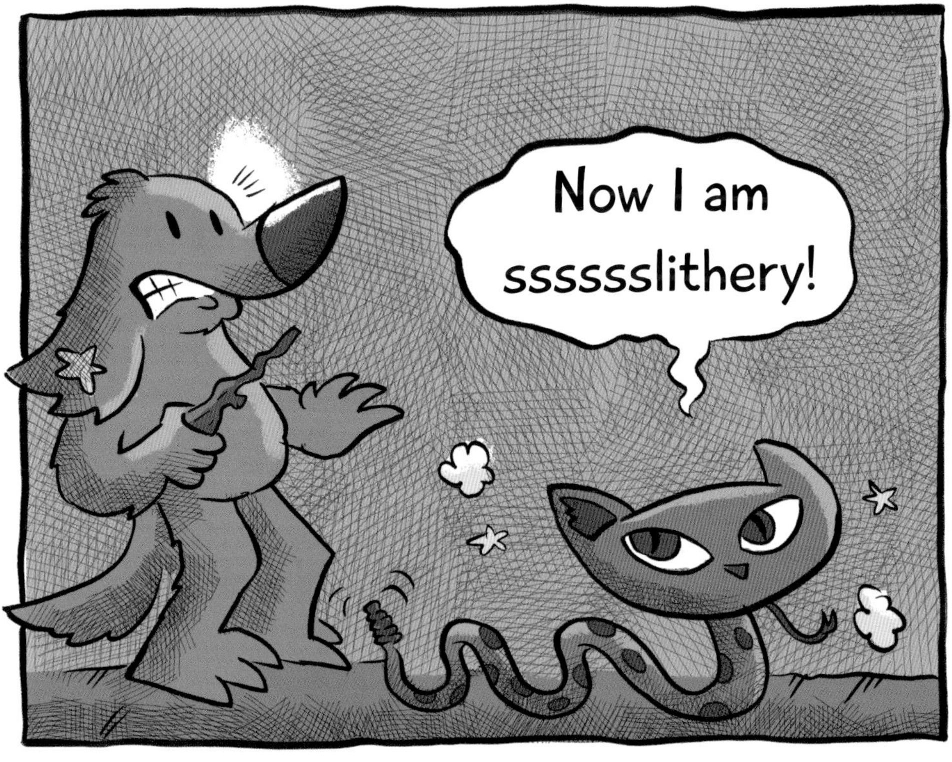
Now I am ssssslithery!

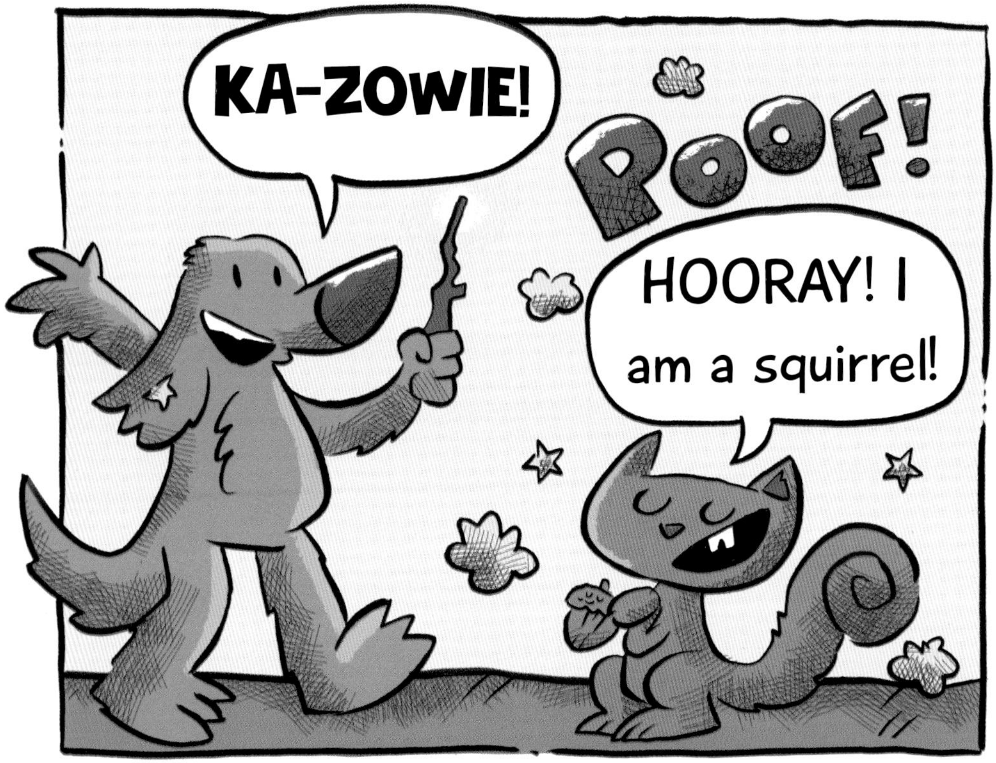
KA-ZOWIE!
POOF!
HOORAY! I am a squirrel!

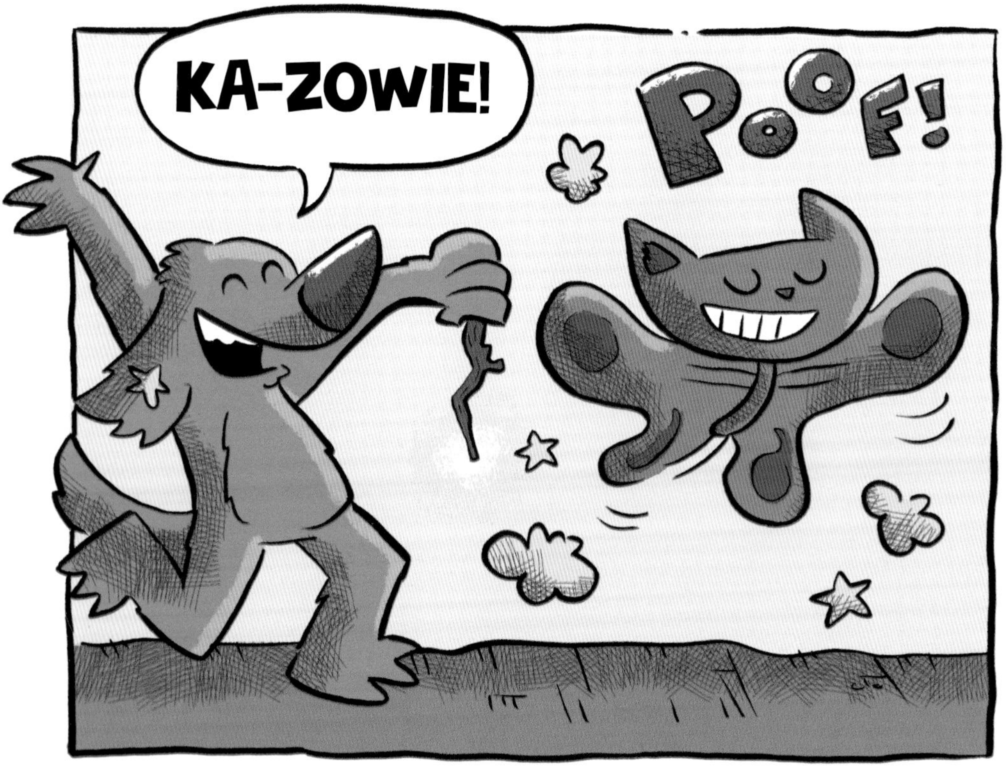
KA-ZOWIE!
POOF!

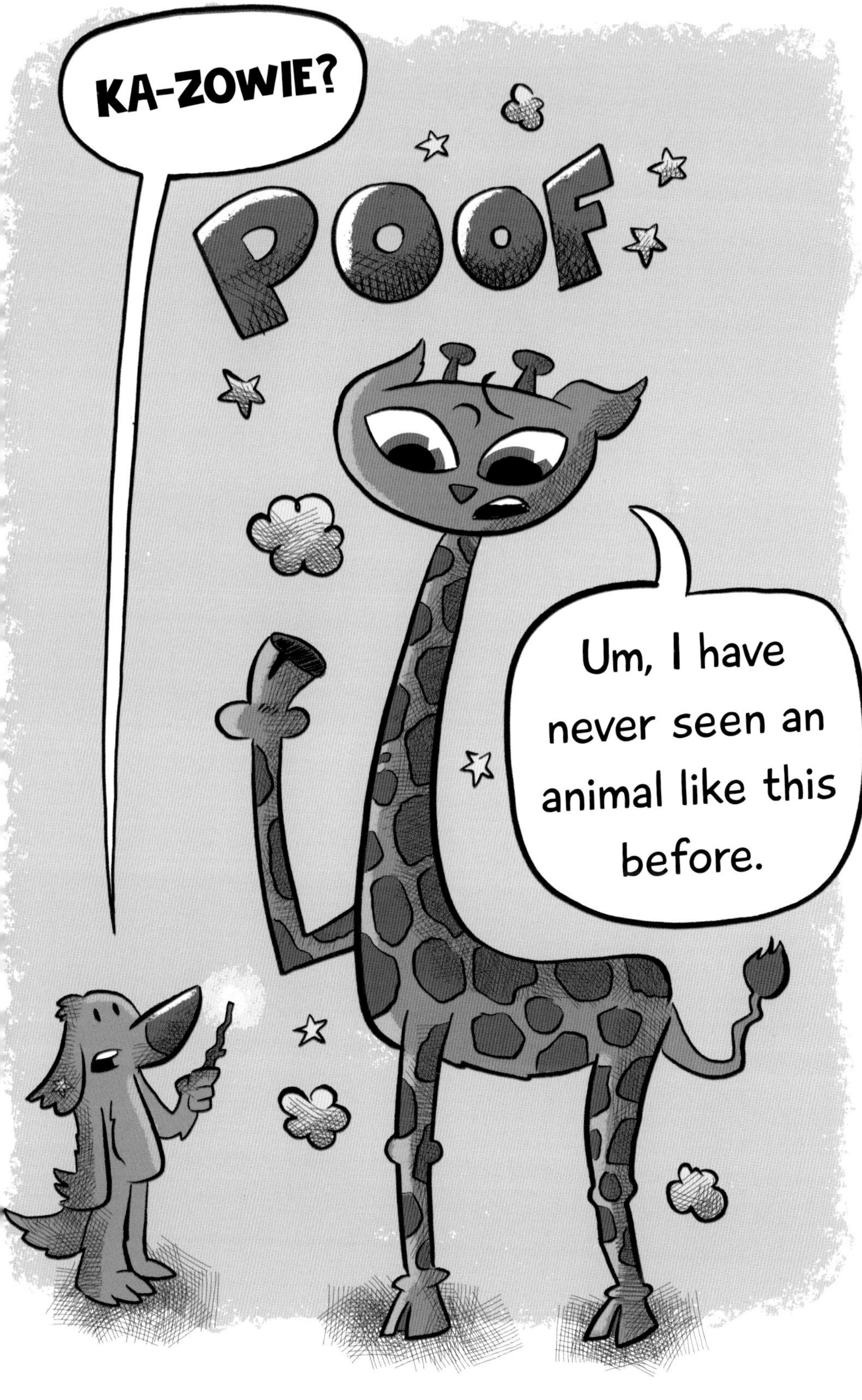
KA-ZOWIE?
POOF
Um, I have never seen an animal like this before.

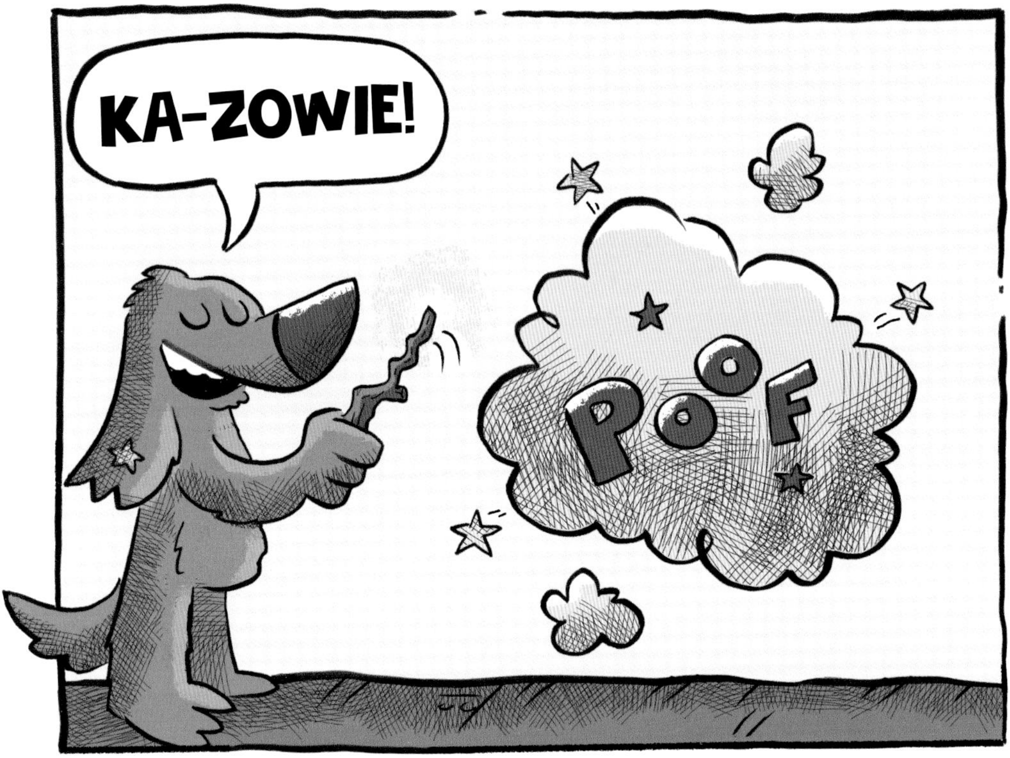
KA-ZOWIE!
POOF

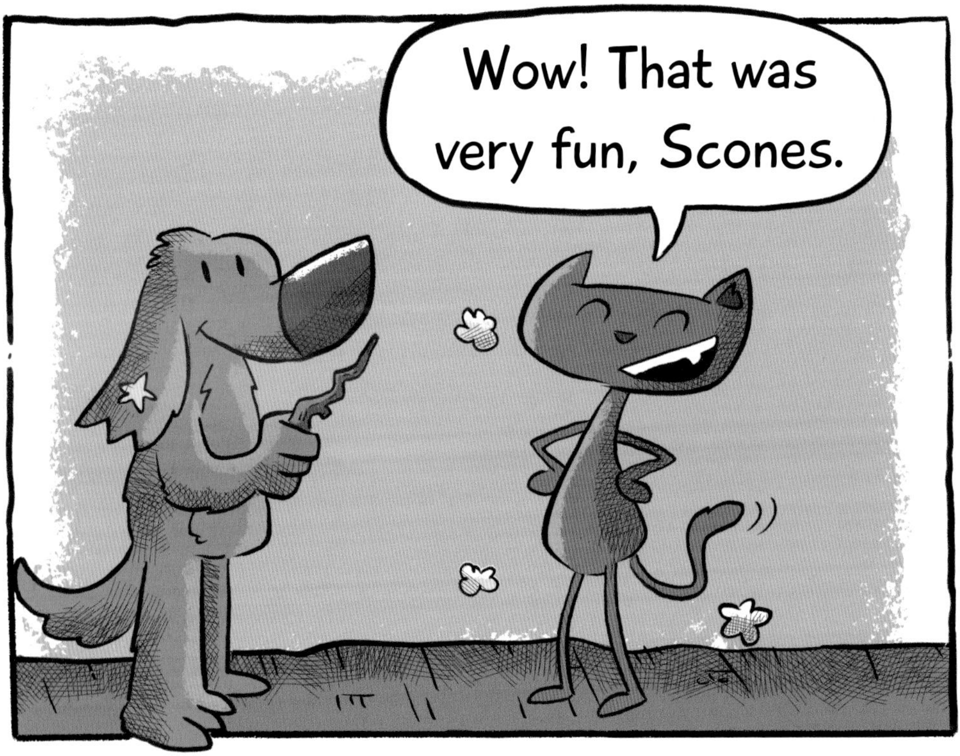
Wow! That was very fun, Scones.

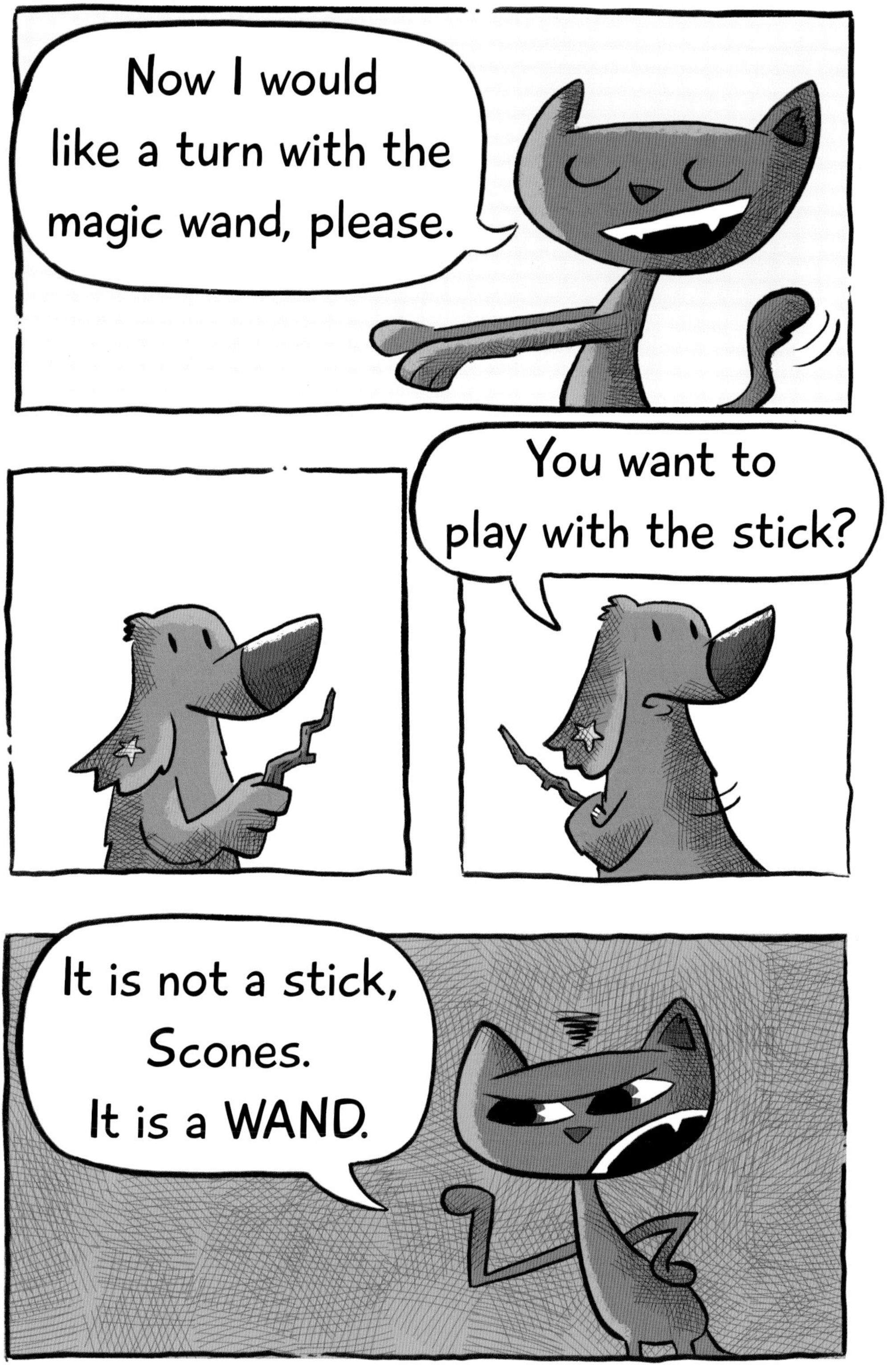
Now I would like a turn with the magic wand, please.
You want to play with the stick?
It is not a stick, Scones. It is a WAND.

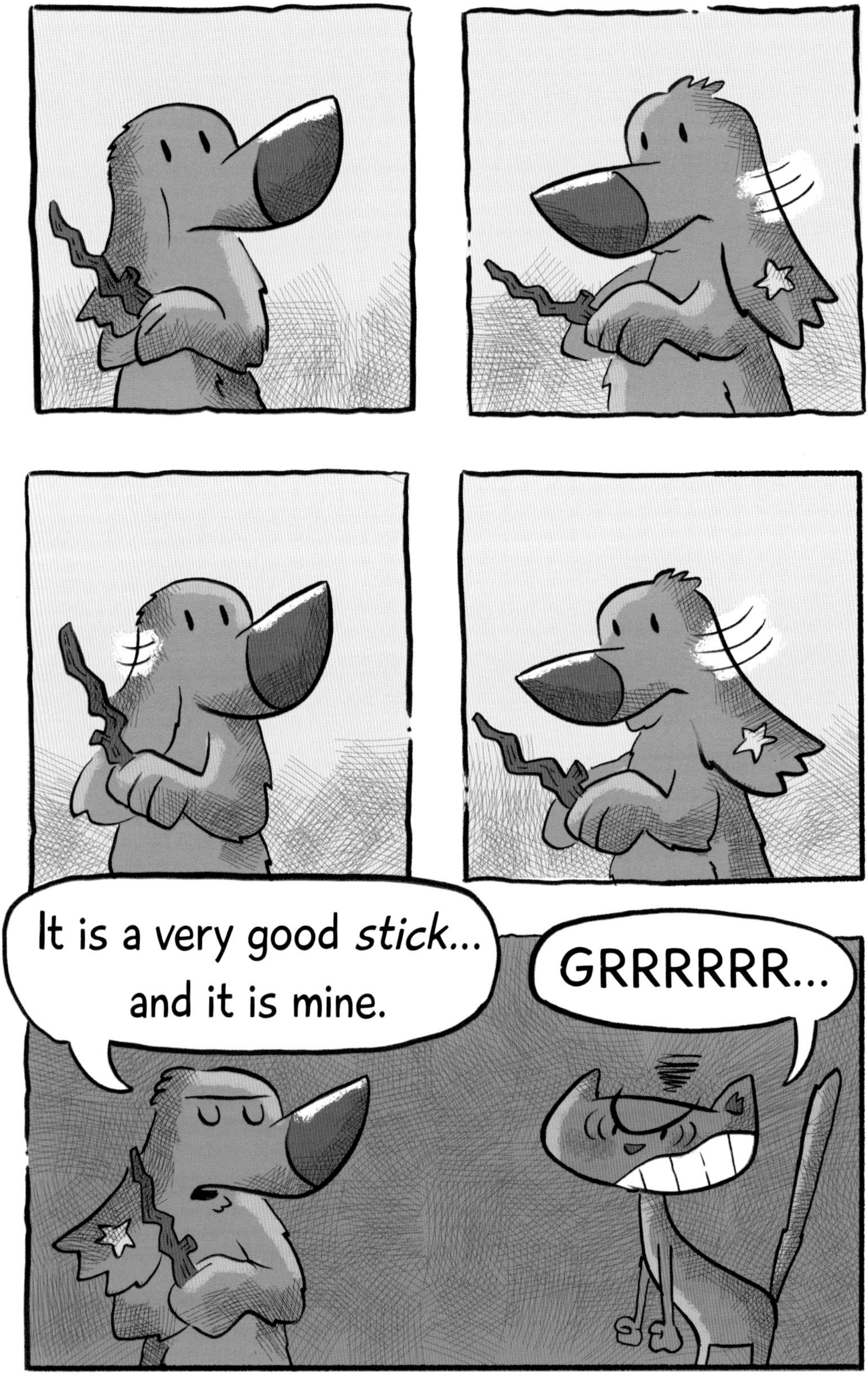
It is a very good *stick*...
and it is mine.
GRRRRRR...

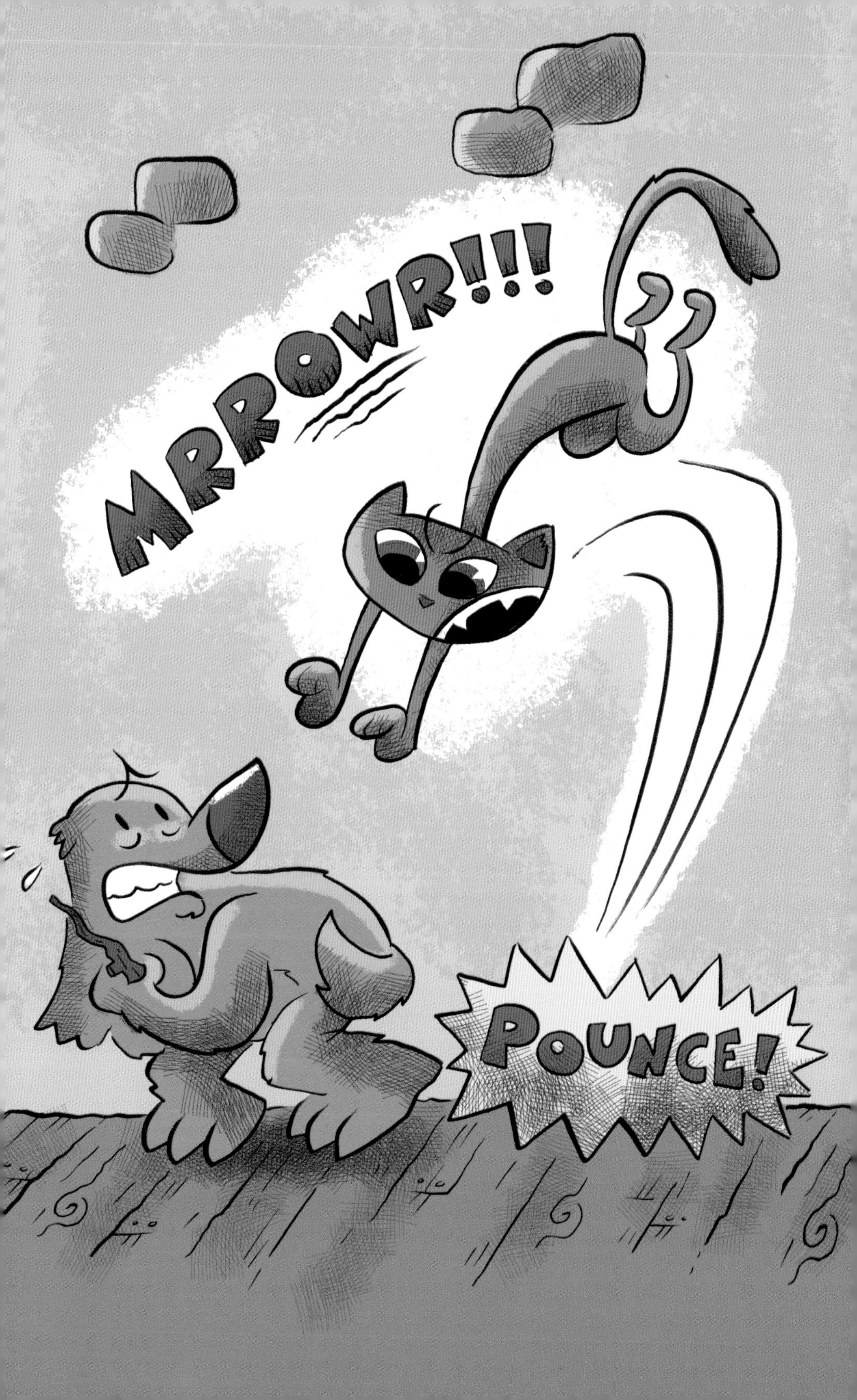
MRROWR!!!
POUNCE!

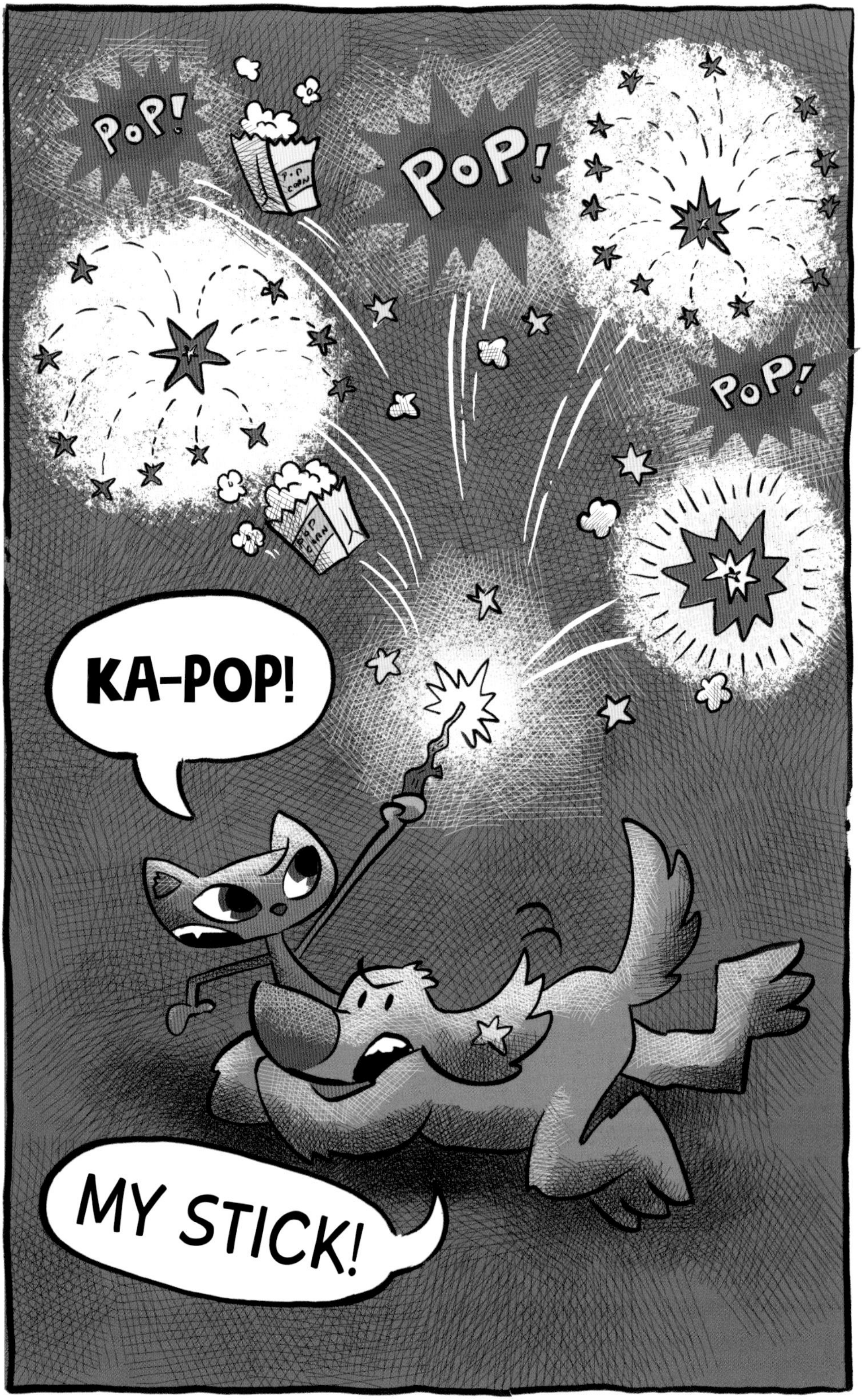
POP!
POP!
POP!
KA-POP!
MY STICK!

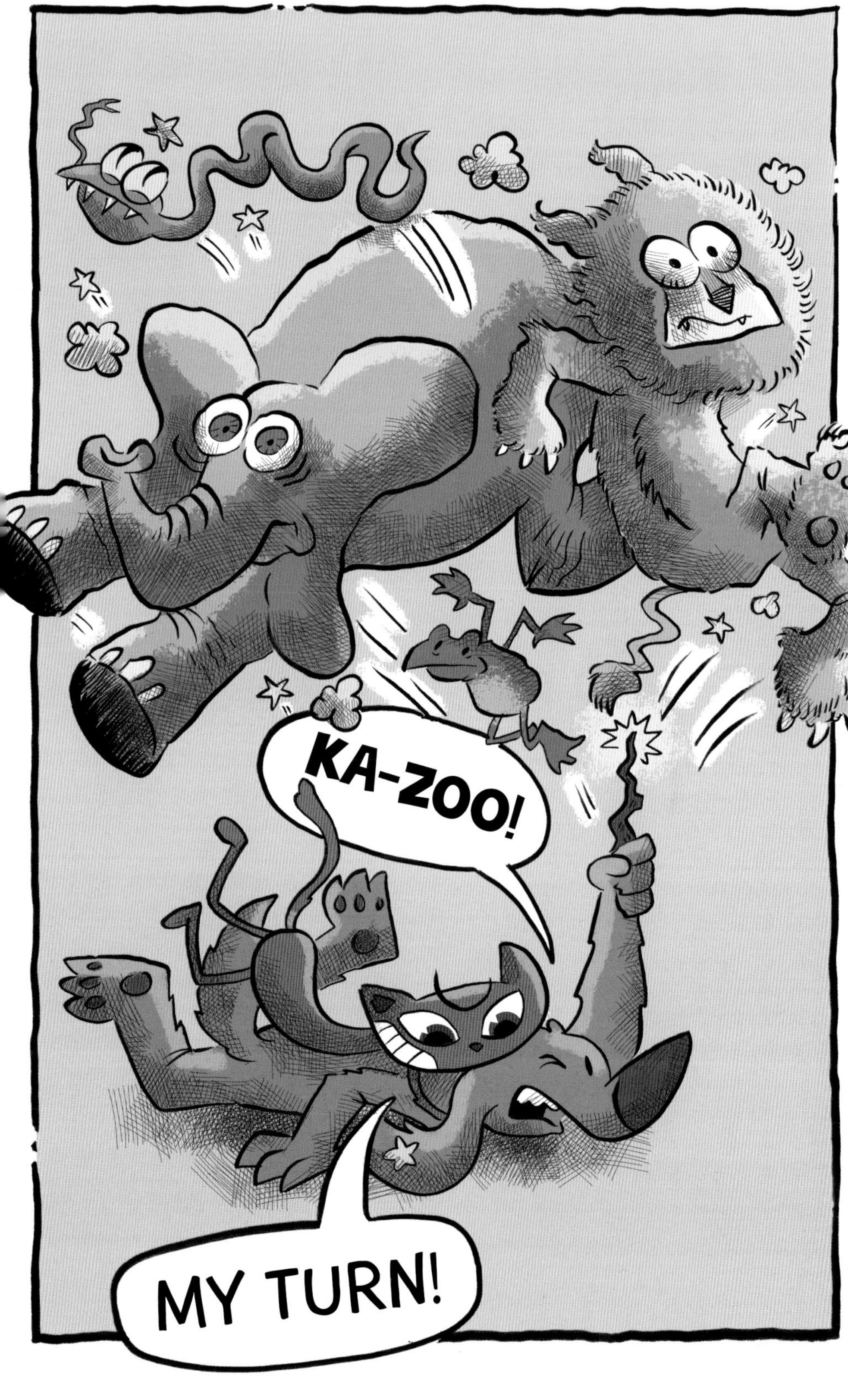
KA-ZOO!
MY TURN!

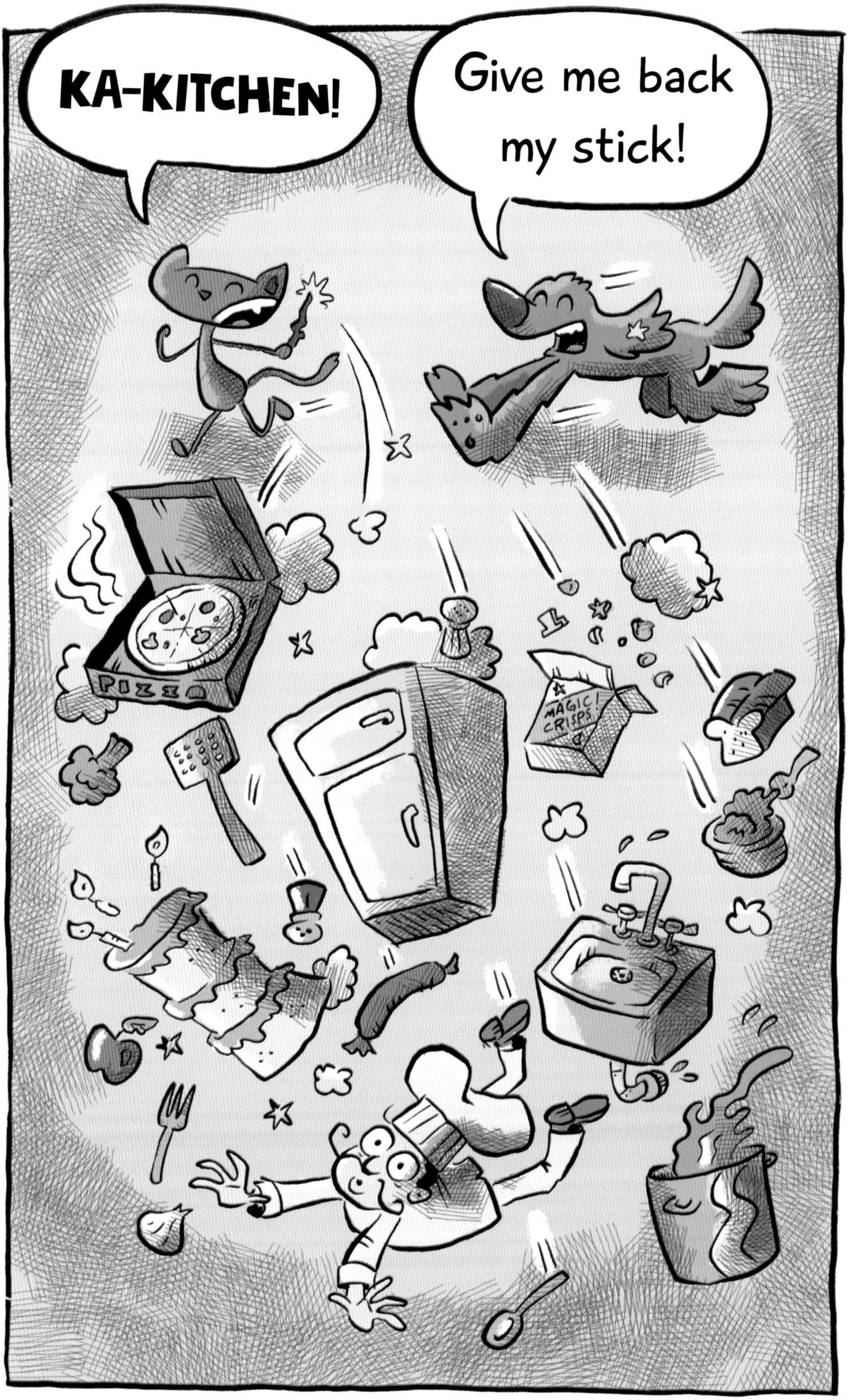
KA-KITCHEN!
Give me back my stick!
PIZZA
MAGIC CRISPS

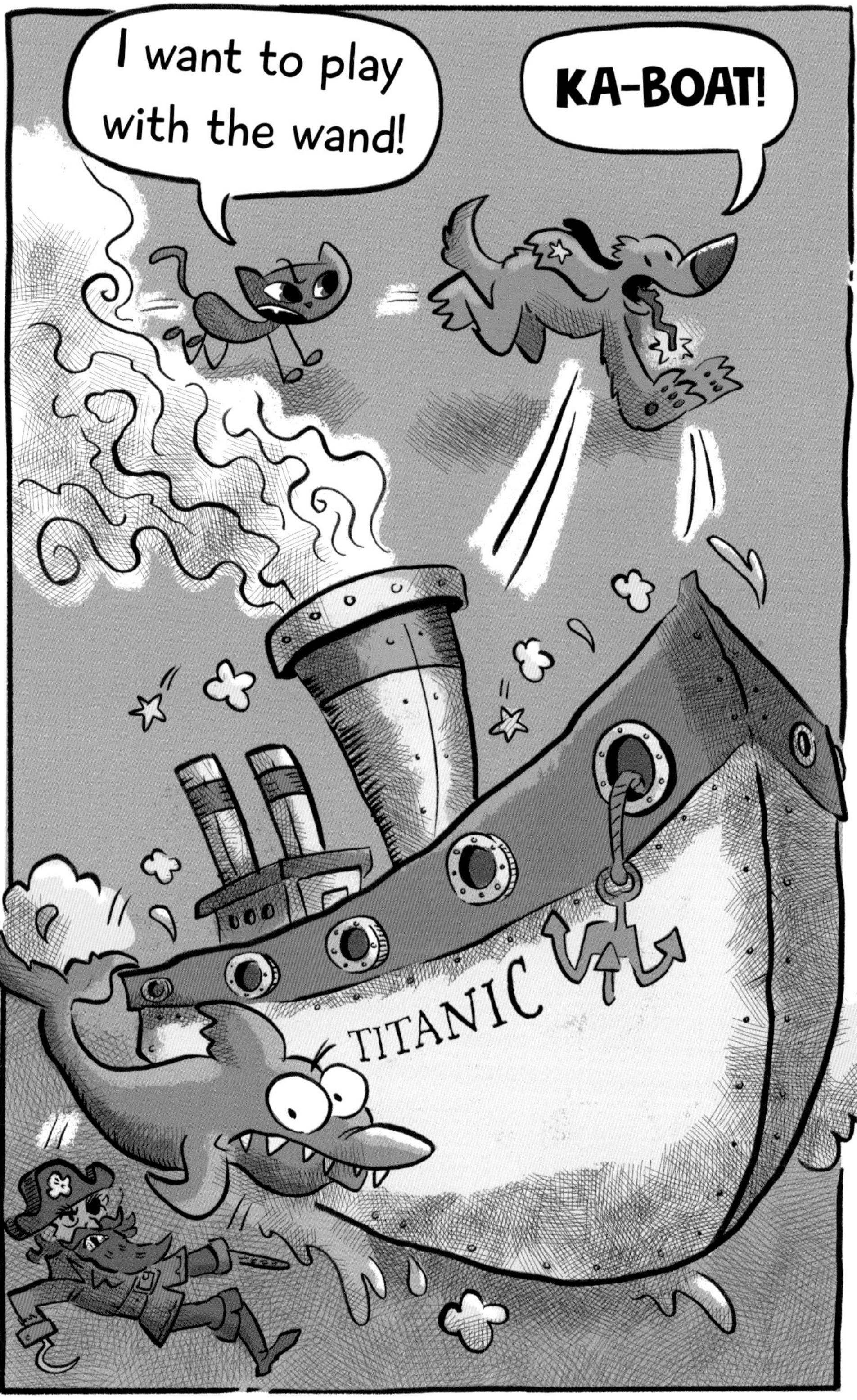
I want to play with the wand!
KA-BOAT!
TITANIC

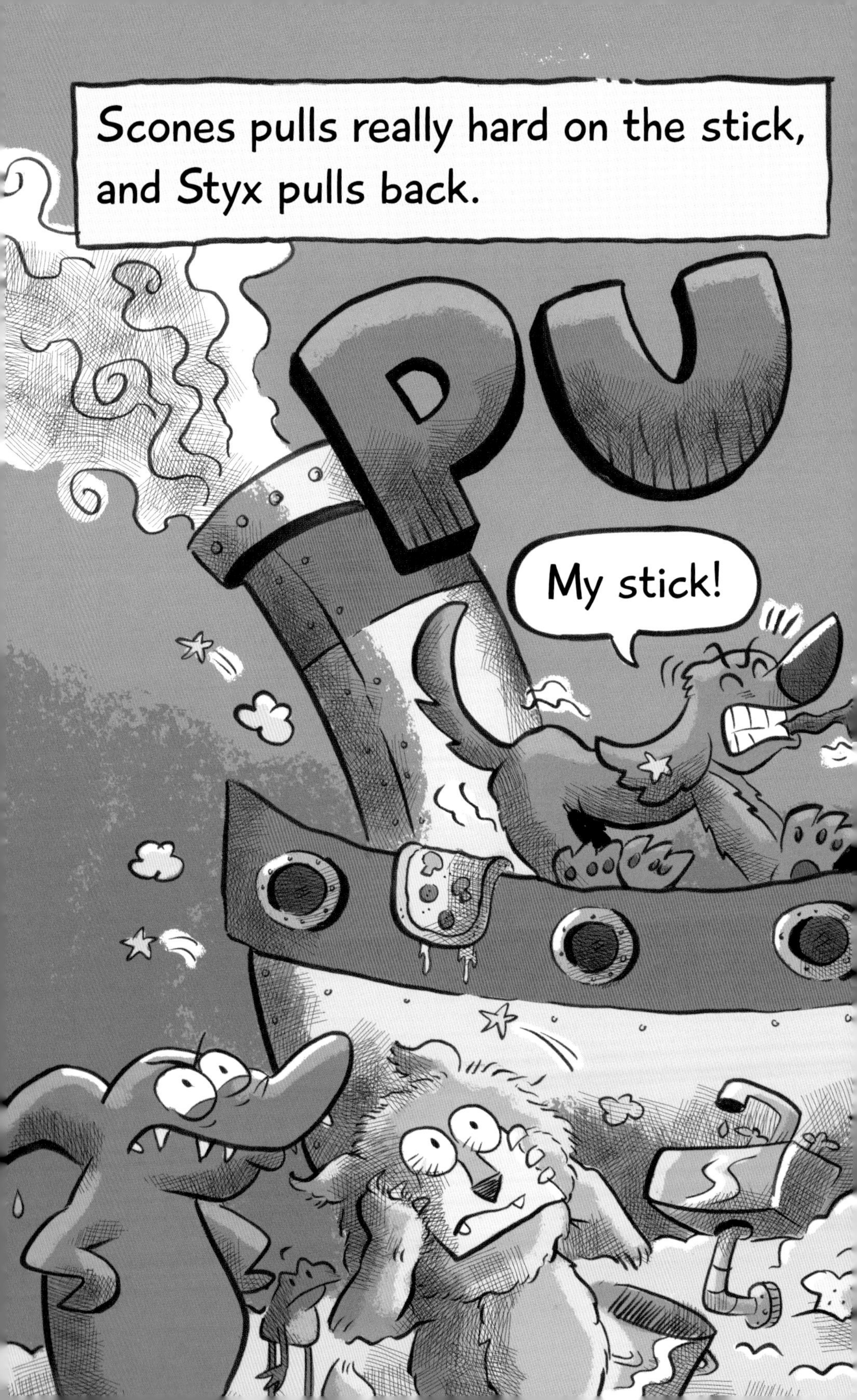
Scones pulls really hard on the stick, and Styx pulls back.
PU
My stick!

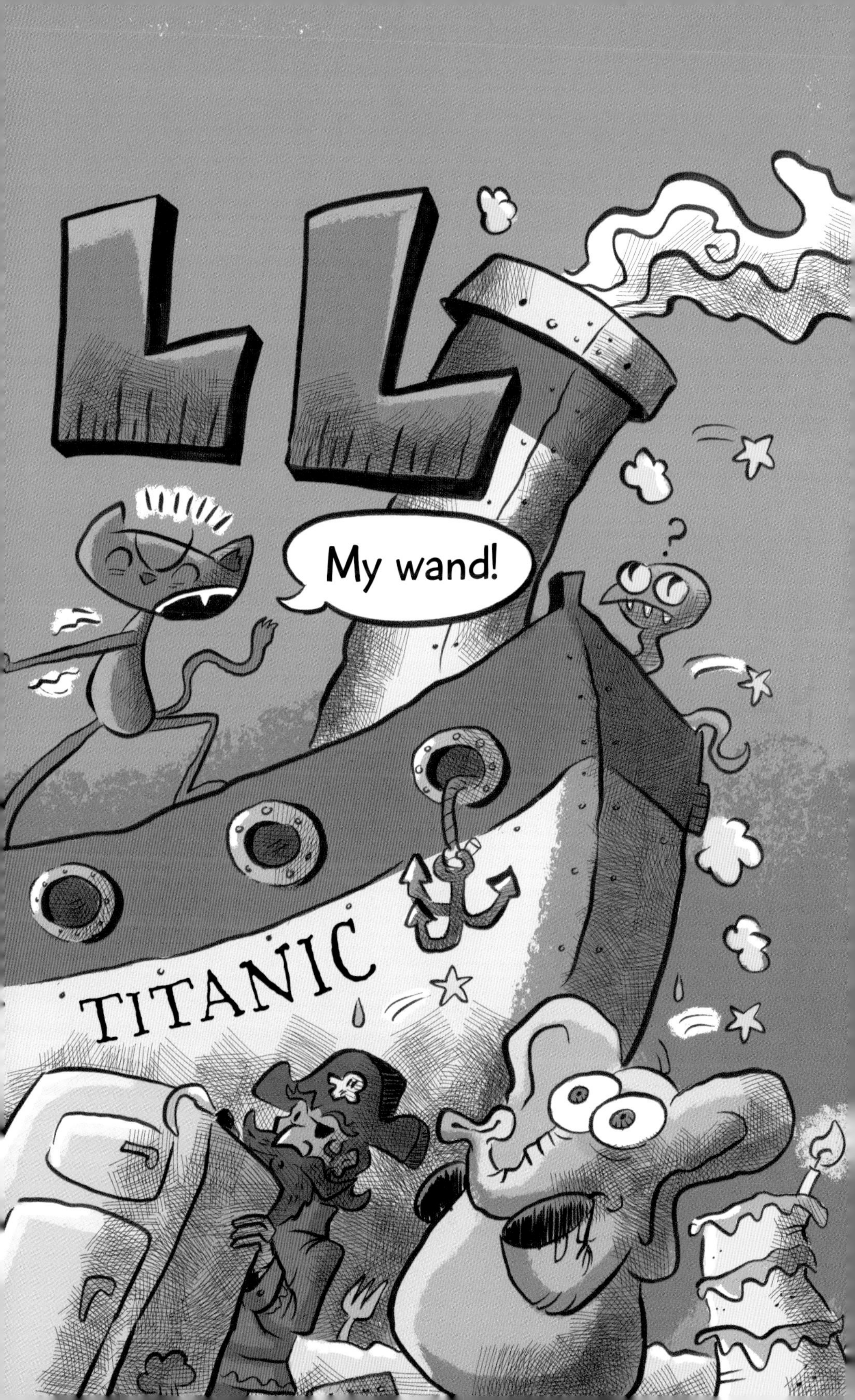

LL
My wand!
TITANIC

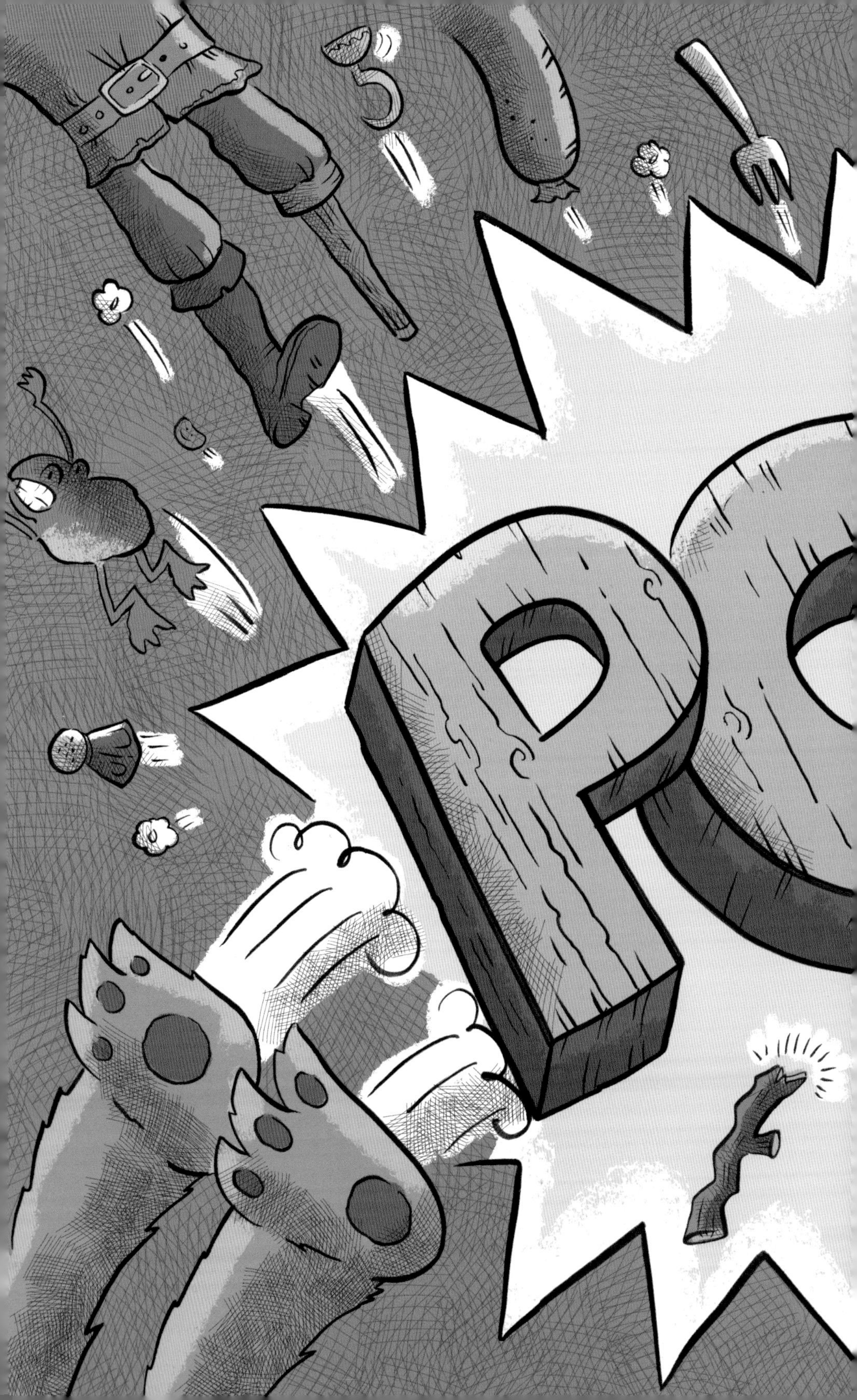
PO

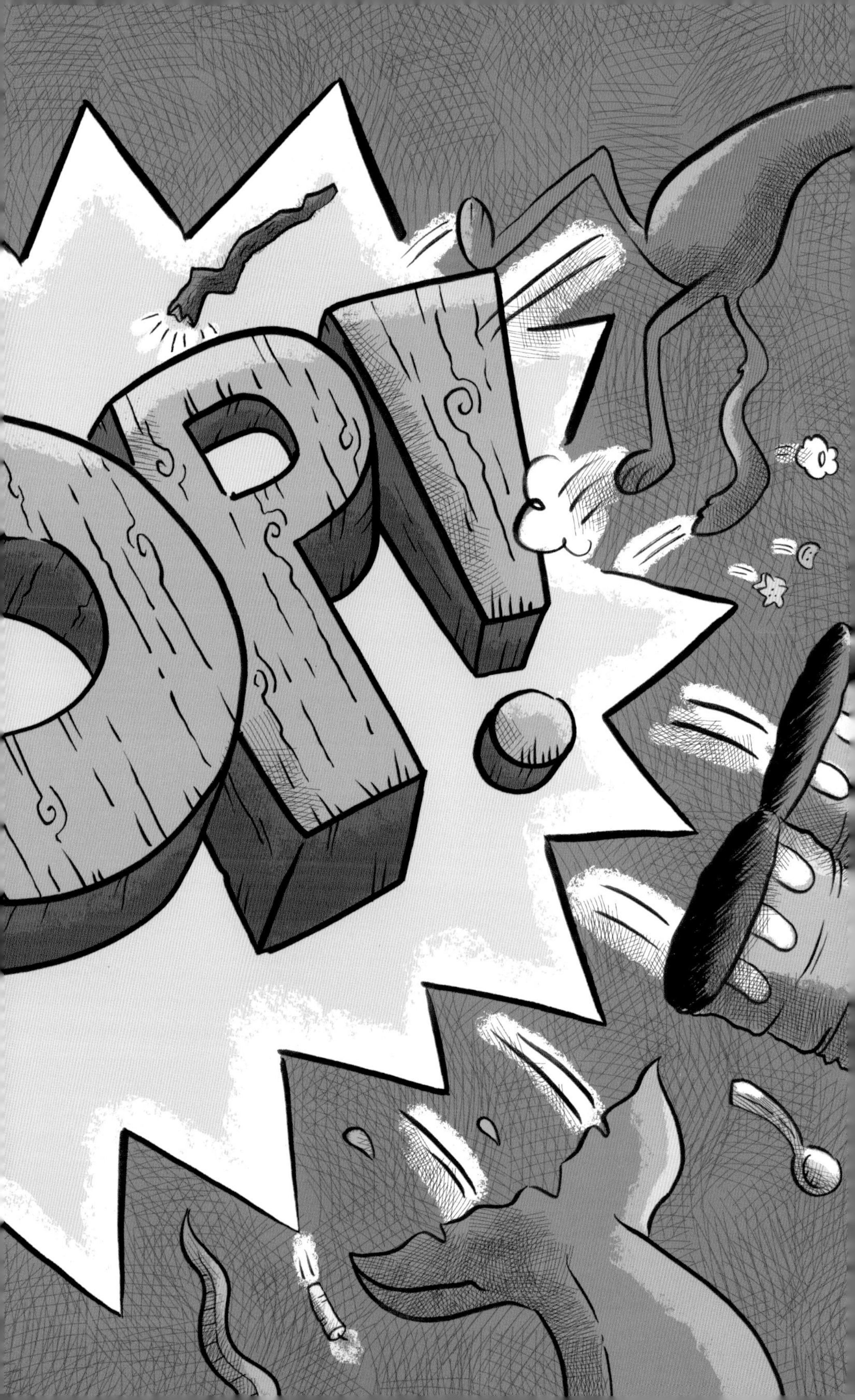

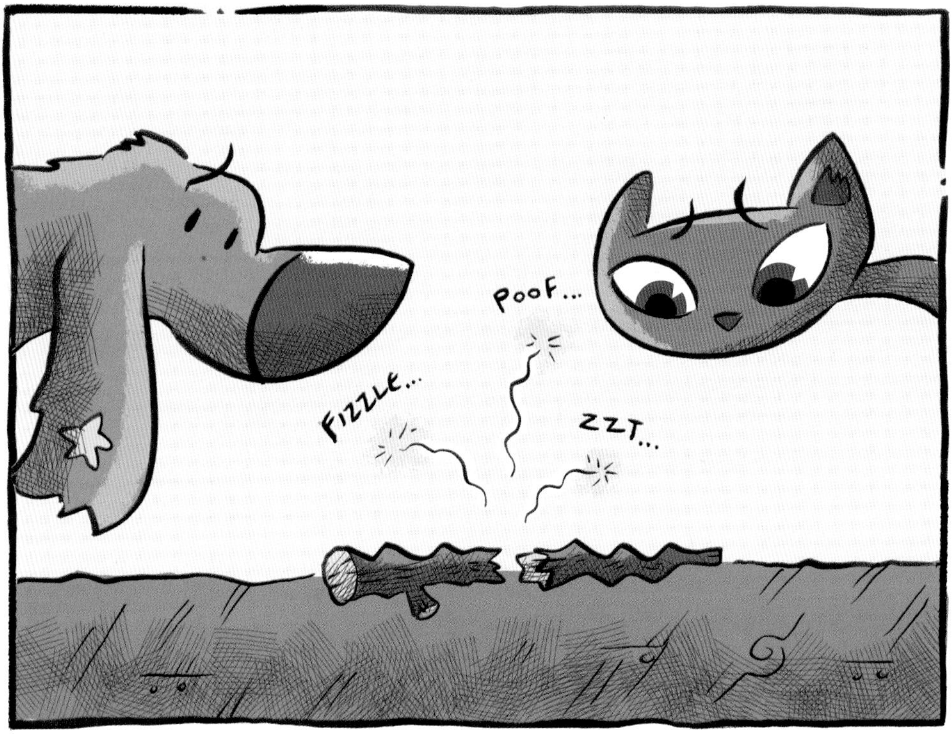
POOF...
FIZZLE...
ZZT...

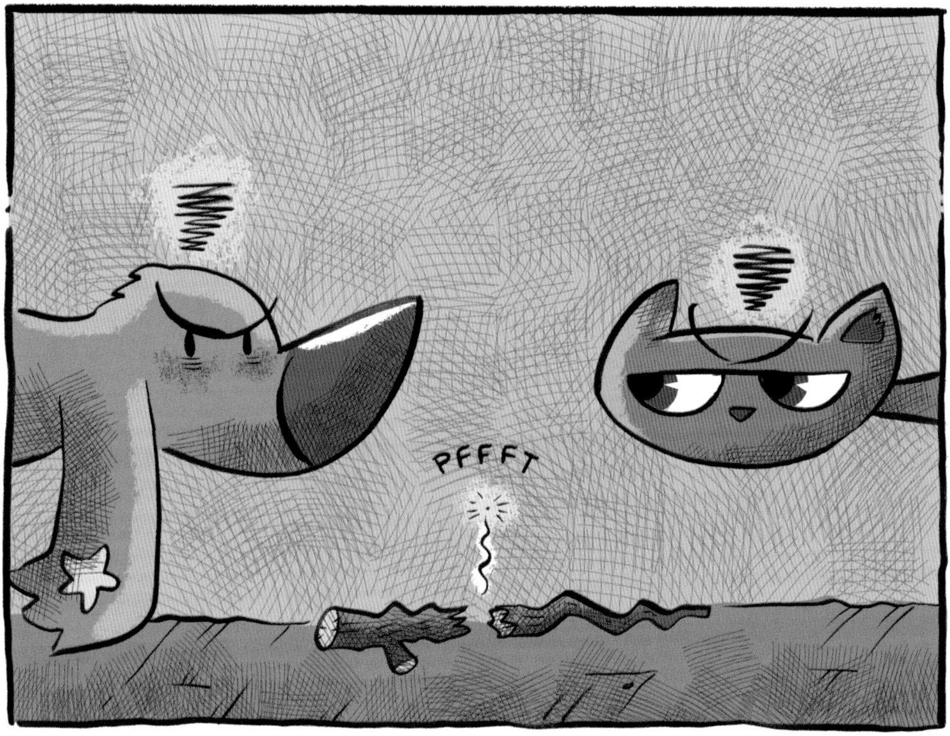
PFFFT

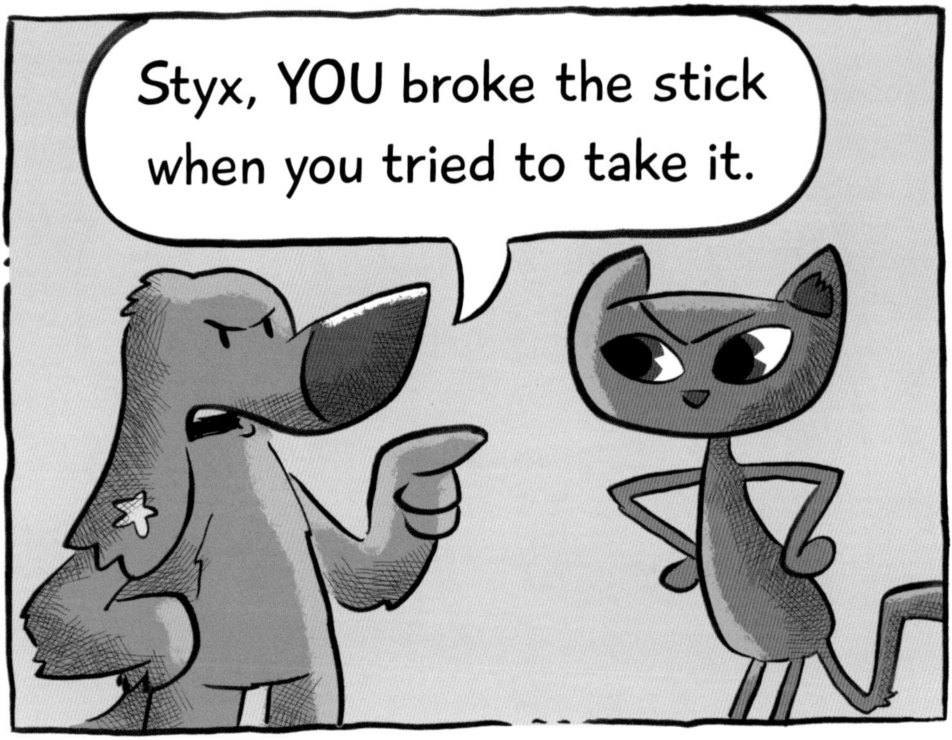
Styx, YOU broke the stick when you tried to take it.

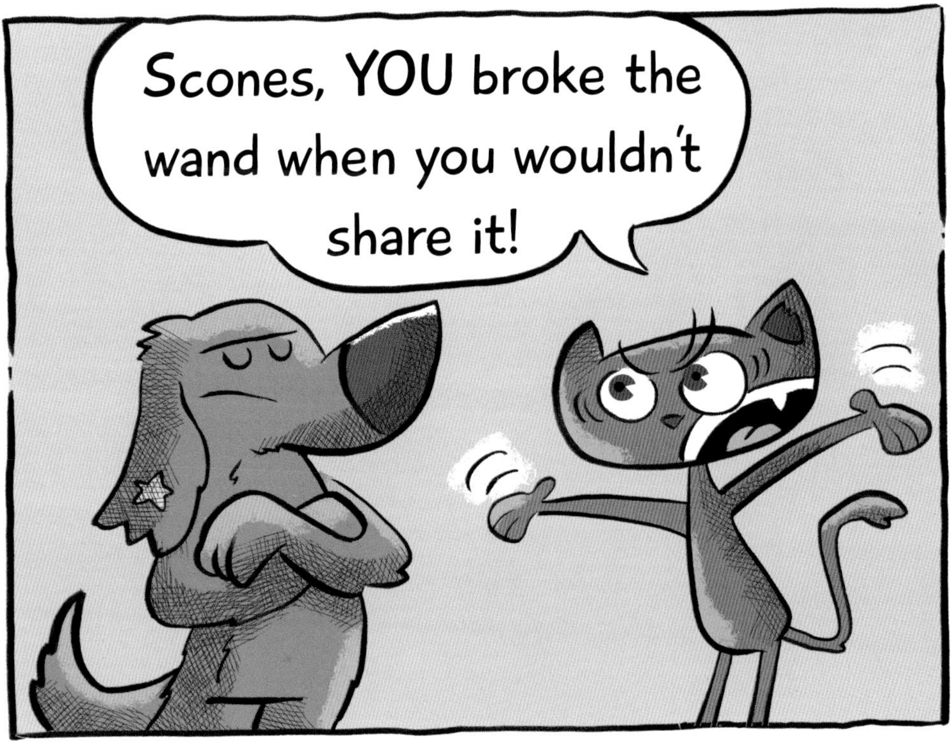
Scones, YOU broke the wand when you wouldn't share it!

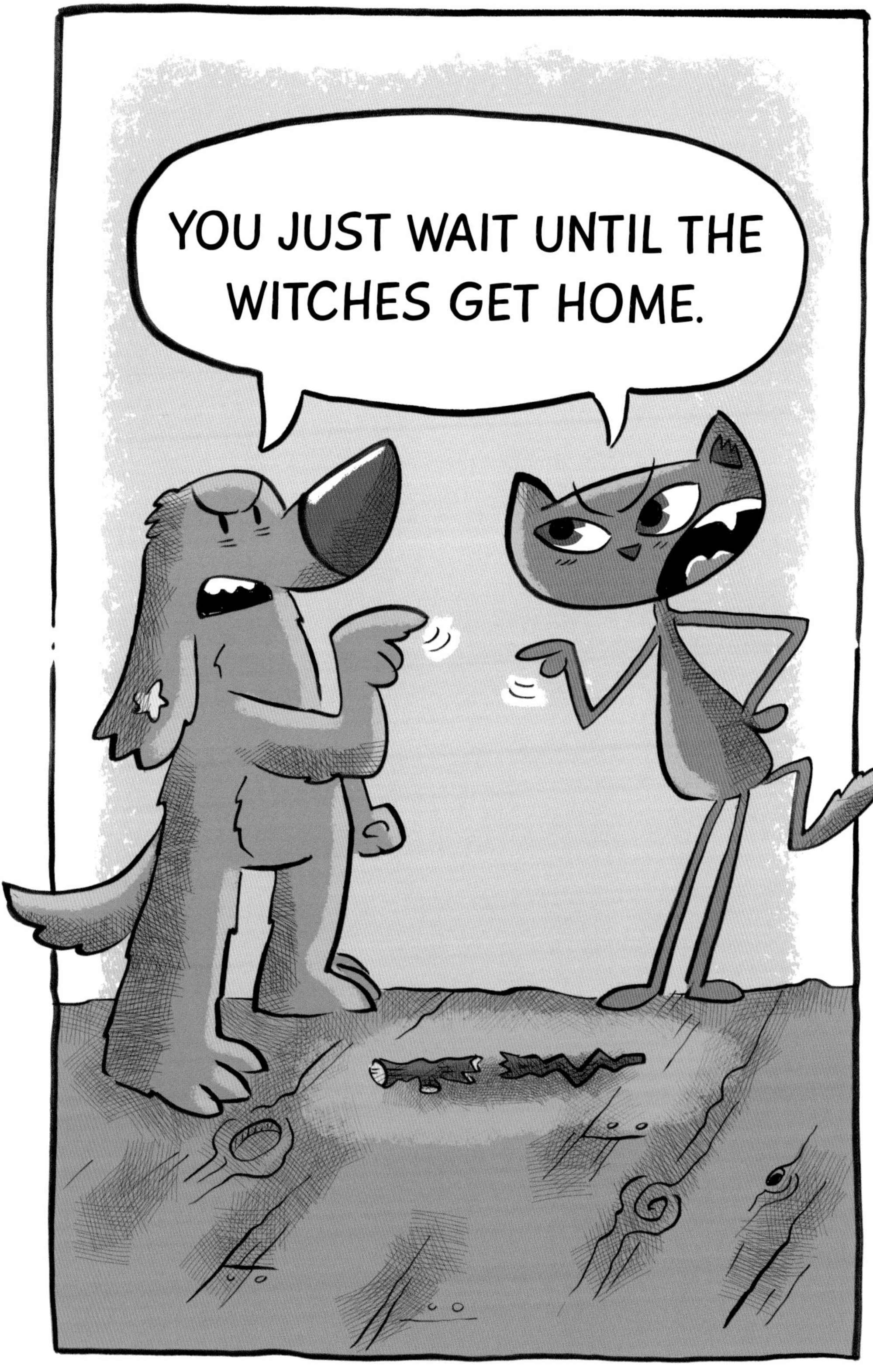
YOU JUST WAIT UNTIL THE WITCHES GET HOME.

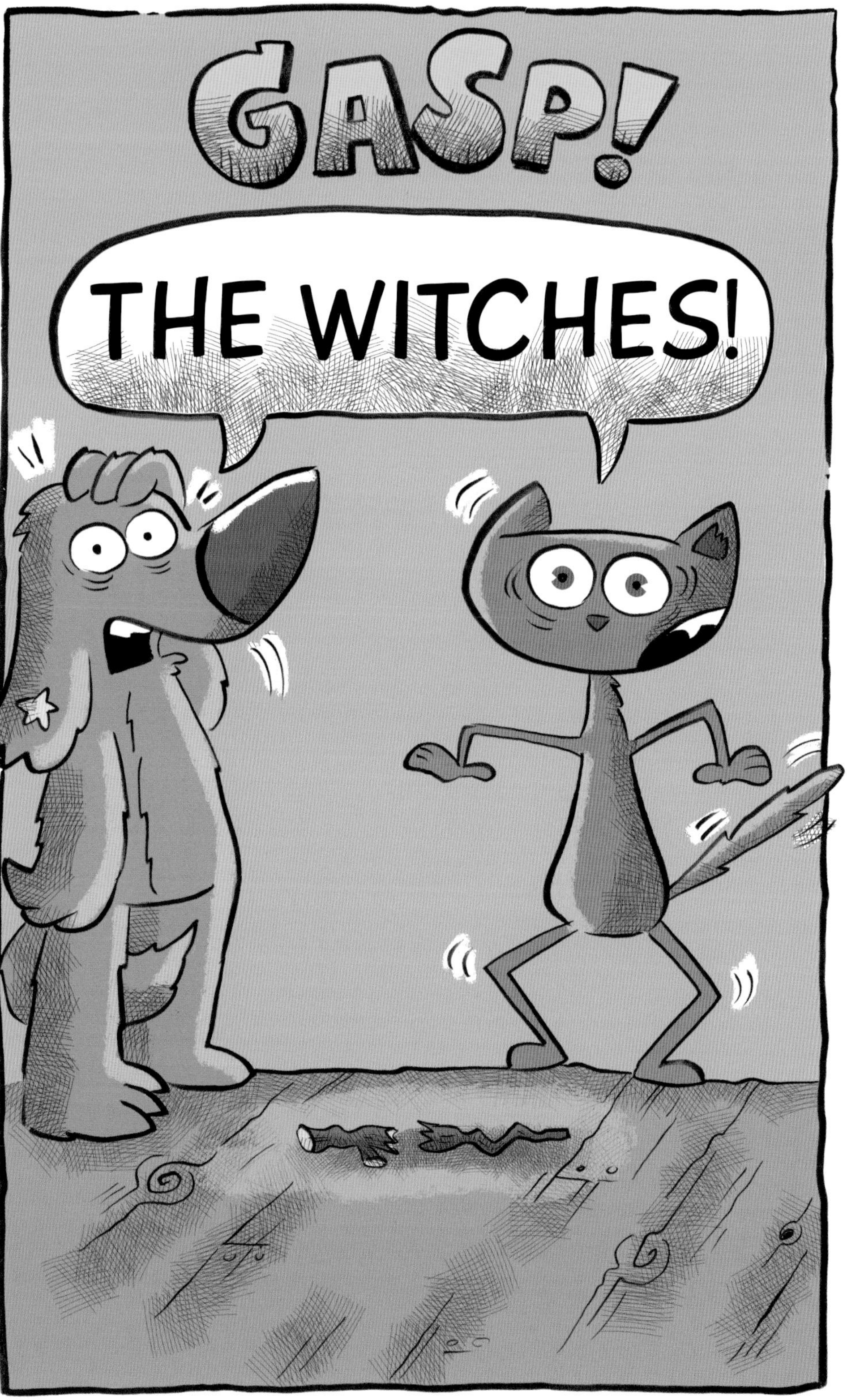
GASP!
THE WITCHES!

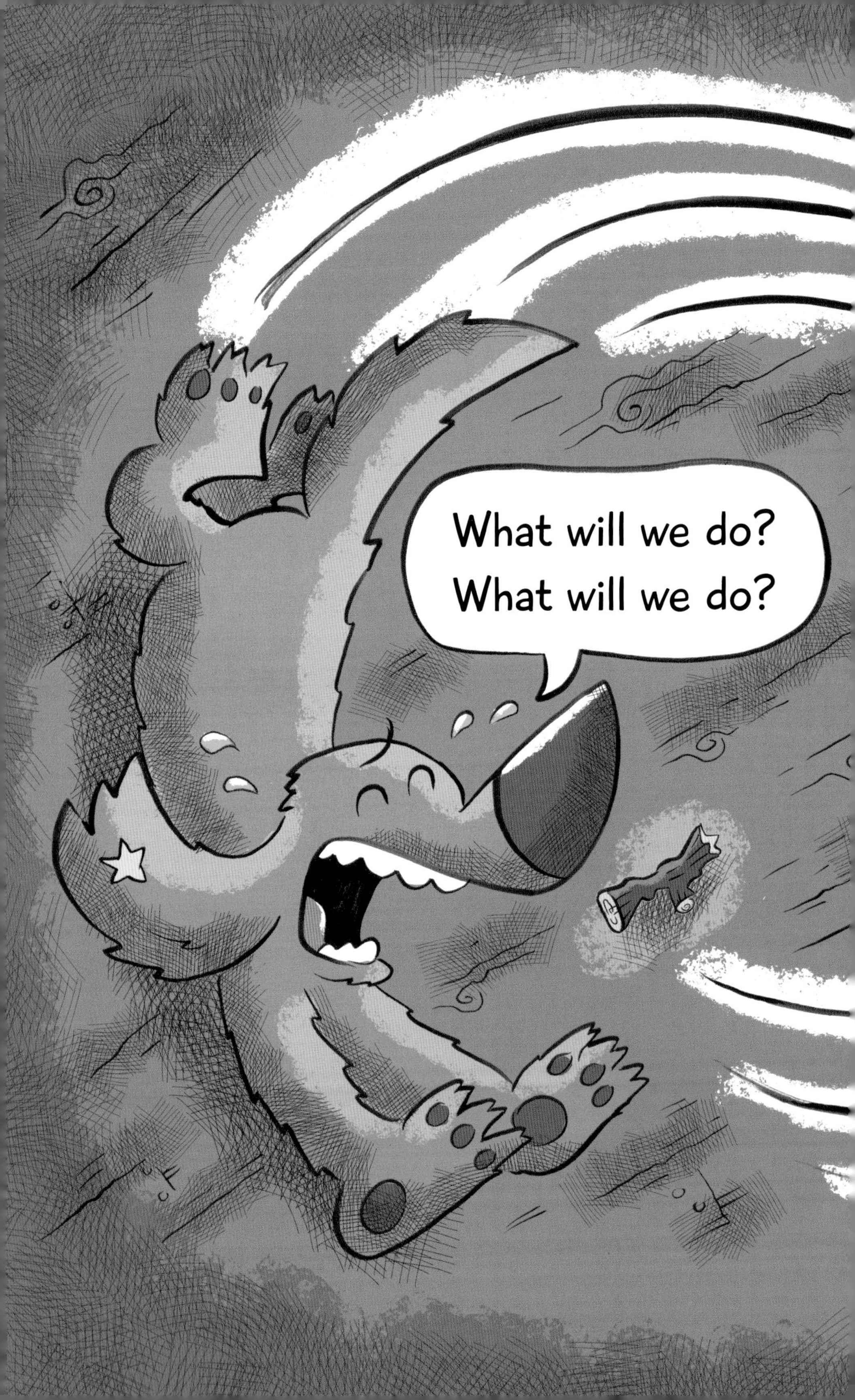
What will we do?
What will we do?

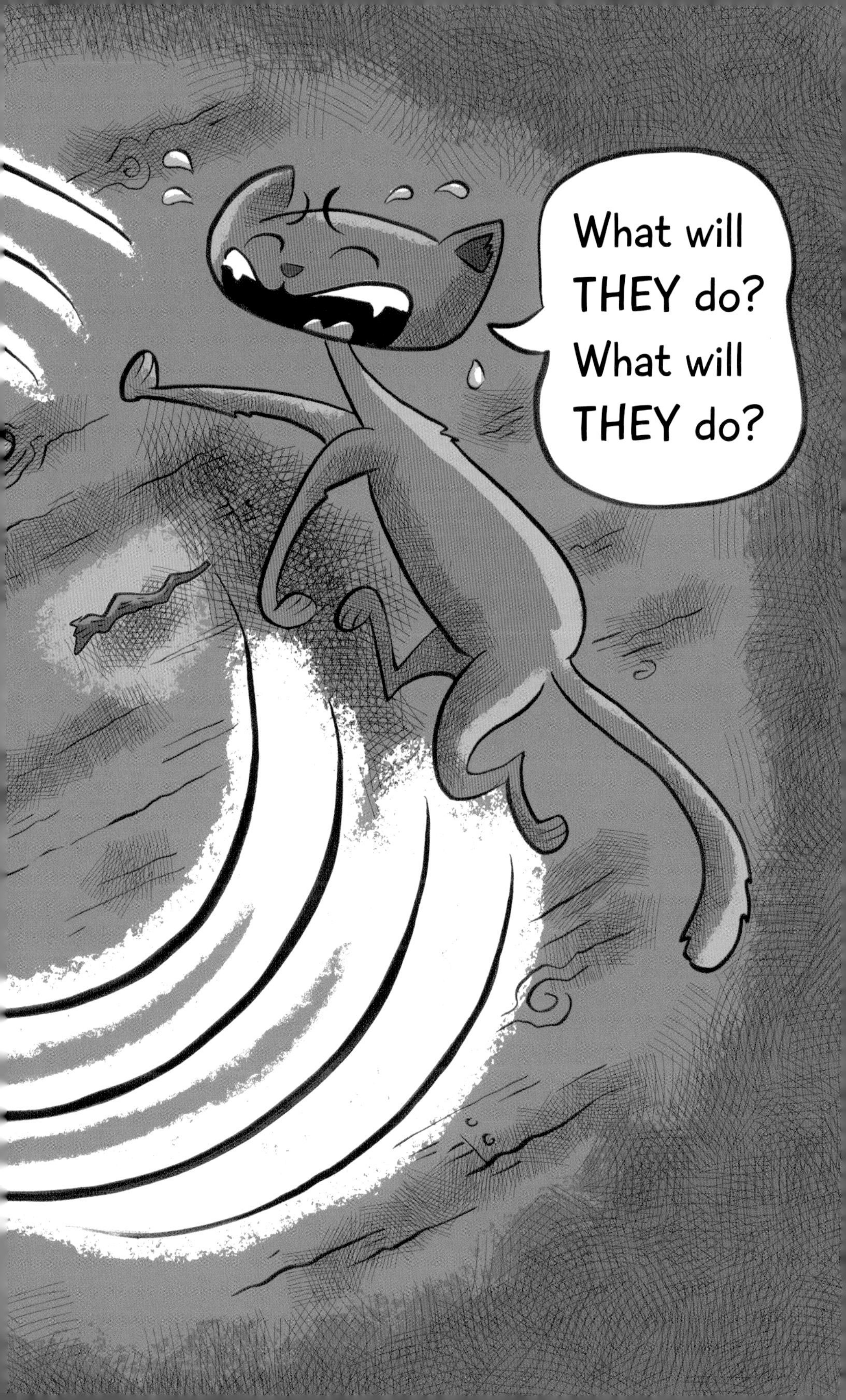
What will THEY do? What will THEY do?

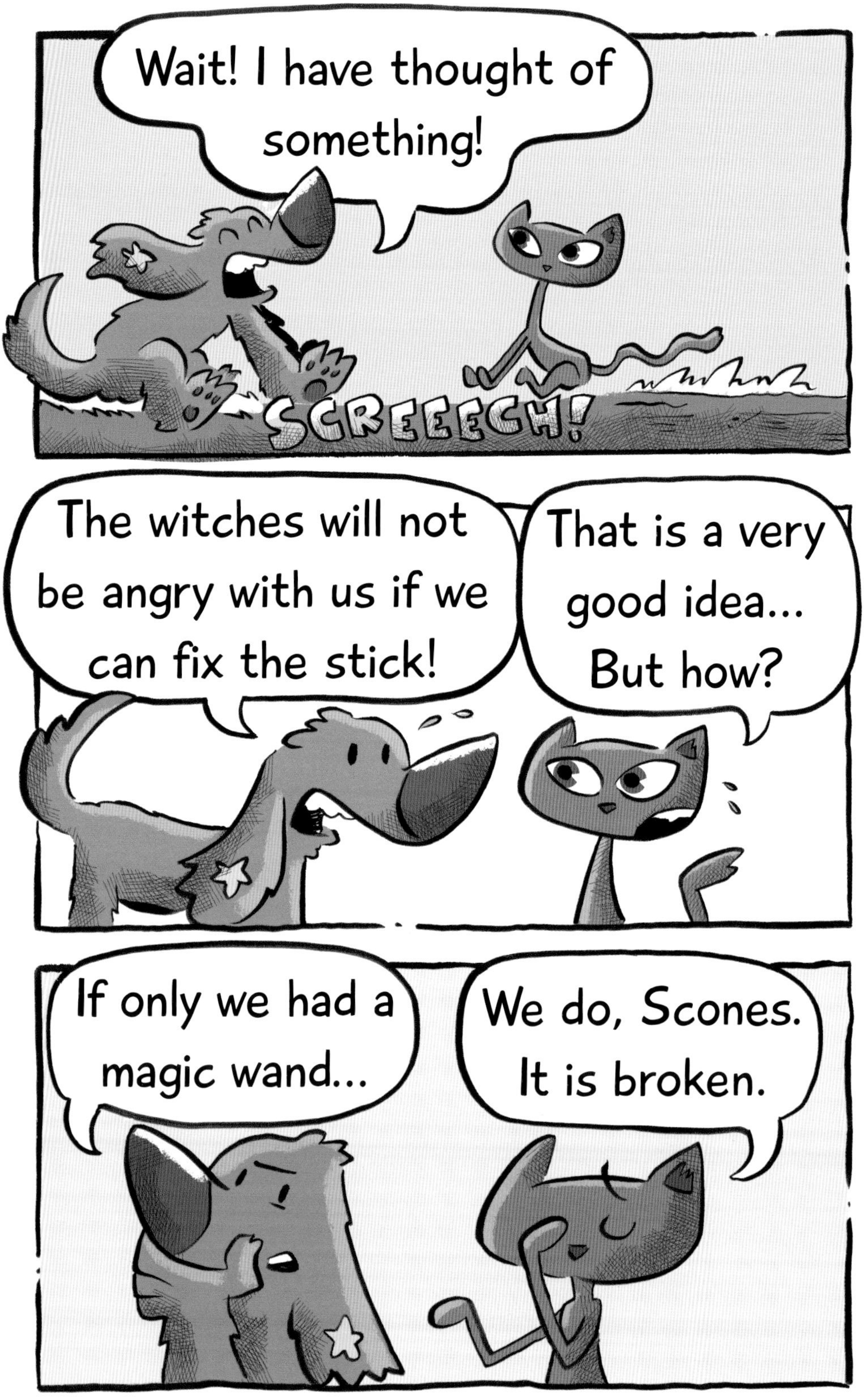
Wait! I have thought of something!
SCREEECH!
The witches will not be angry with us if we can fix the stick!
That is a very good idea... But how?
If only we had a magic wand...
We do, Scones. It is broken.

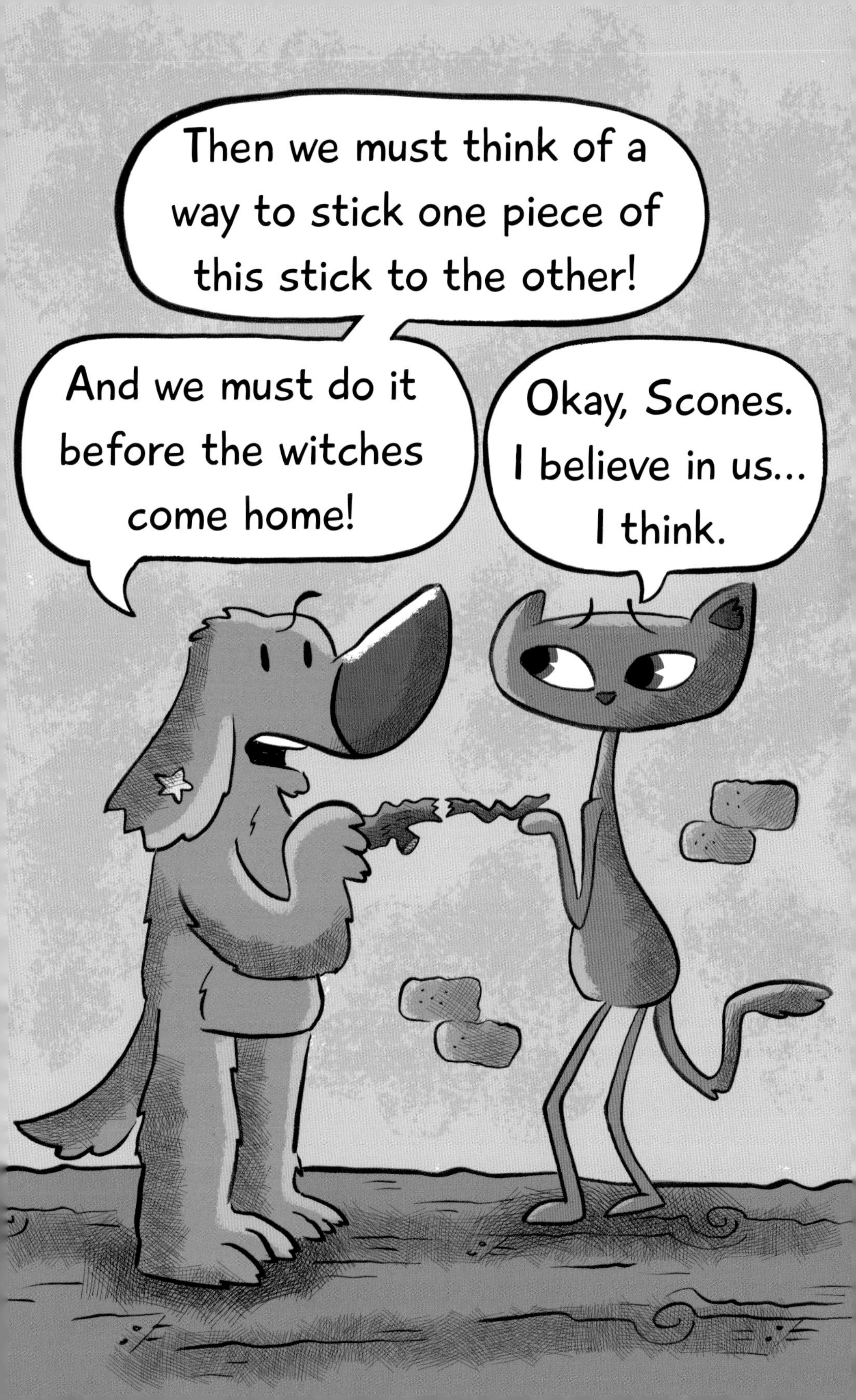
Then we must think of a way to stick one piece of this stick to the other!
And we must do it before the witches come home!
Okay, Scones. I believe in us... I think.

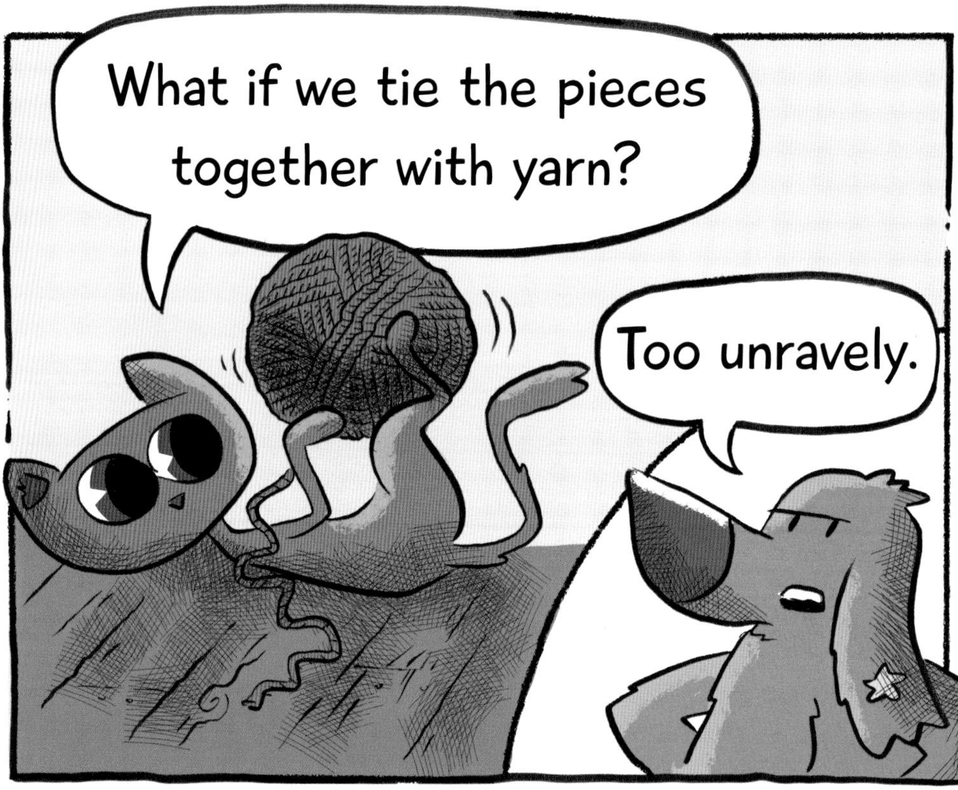
What if we tie the pieces together with yarn?
Too unravely.

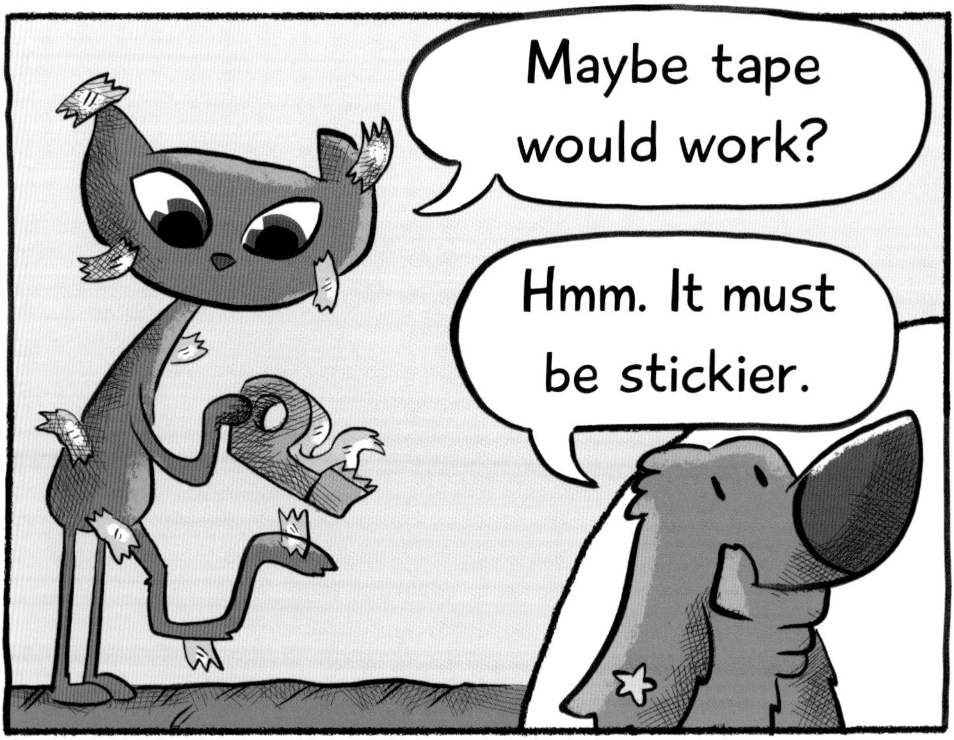
Maybe tape would work?
Hmm. It must be stickier.

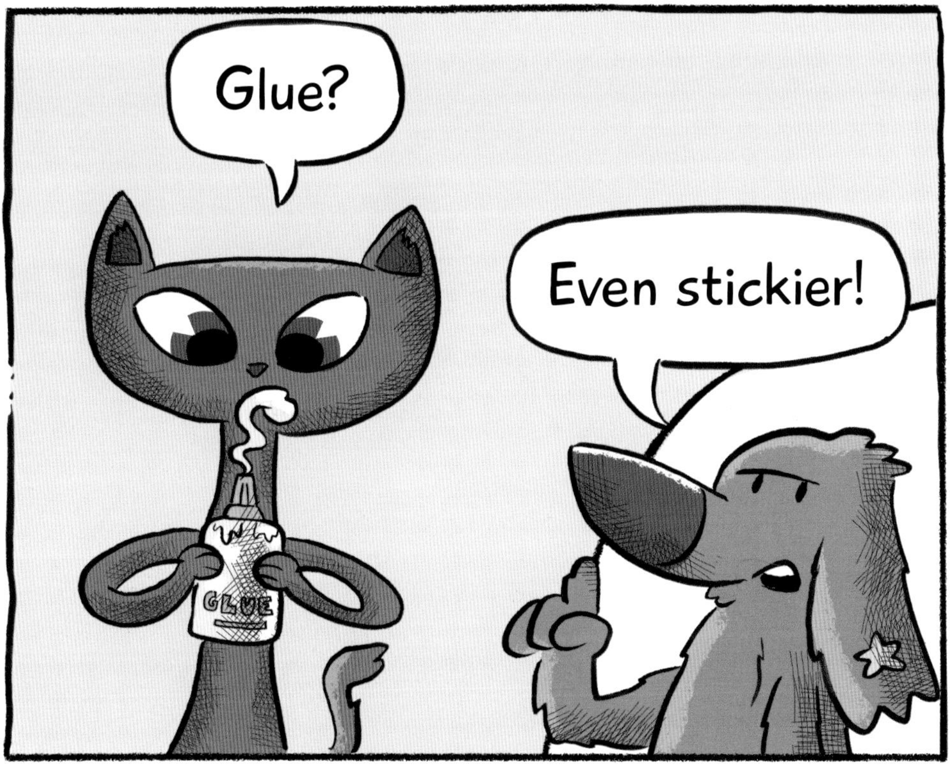
Glue?
Even stickier!
GLUE

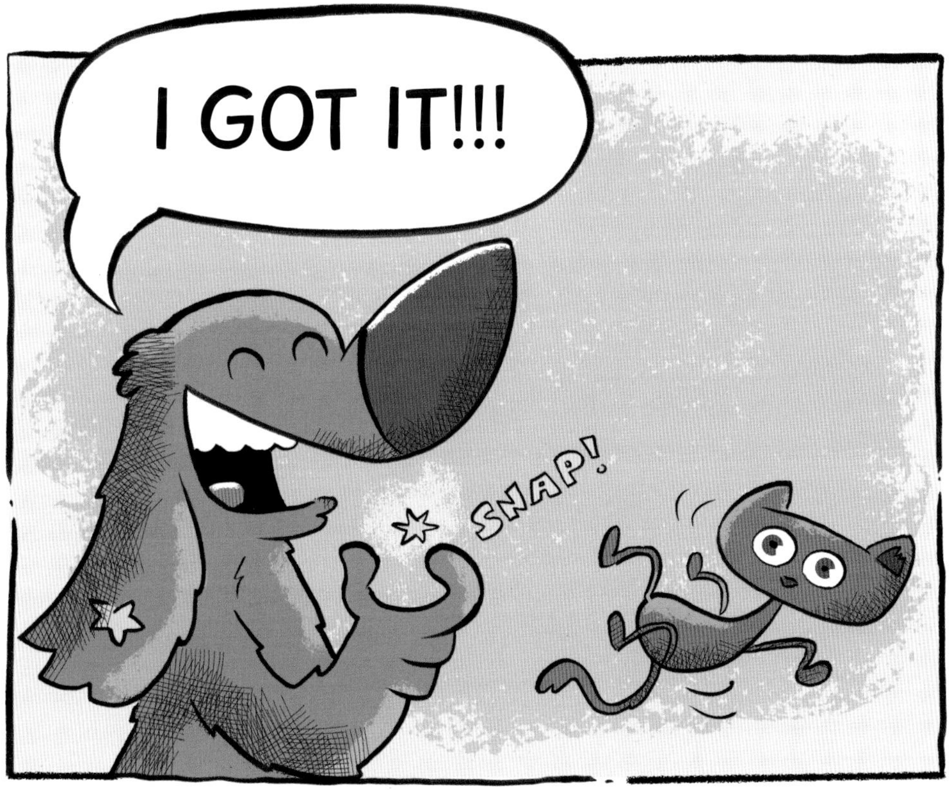
I GOT IT!!!
SNAP!

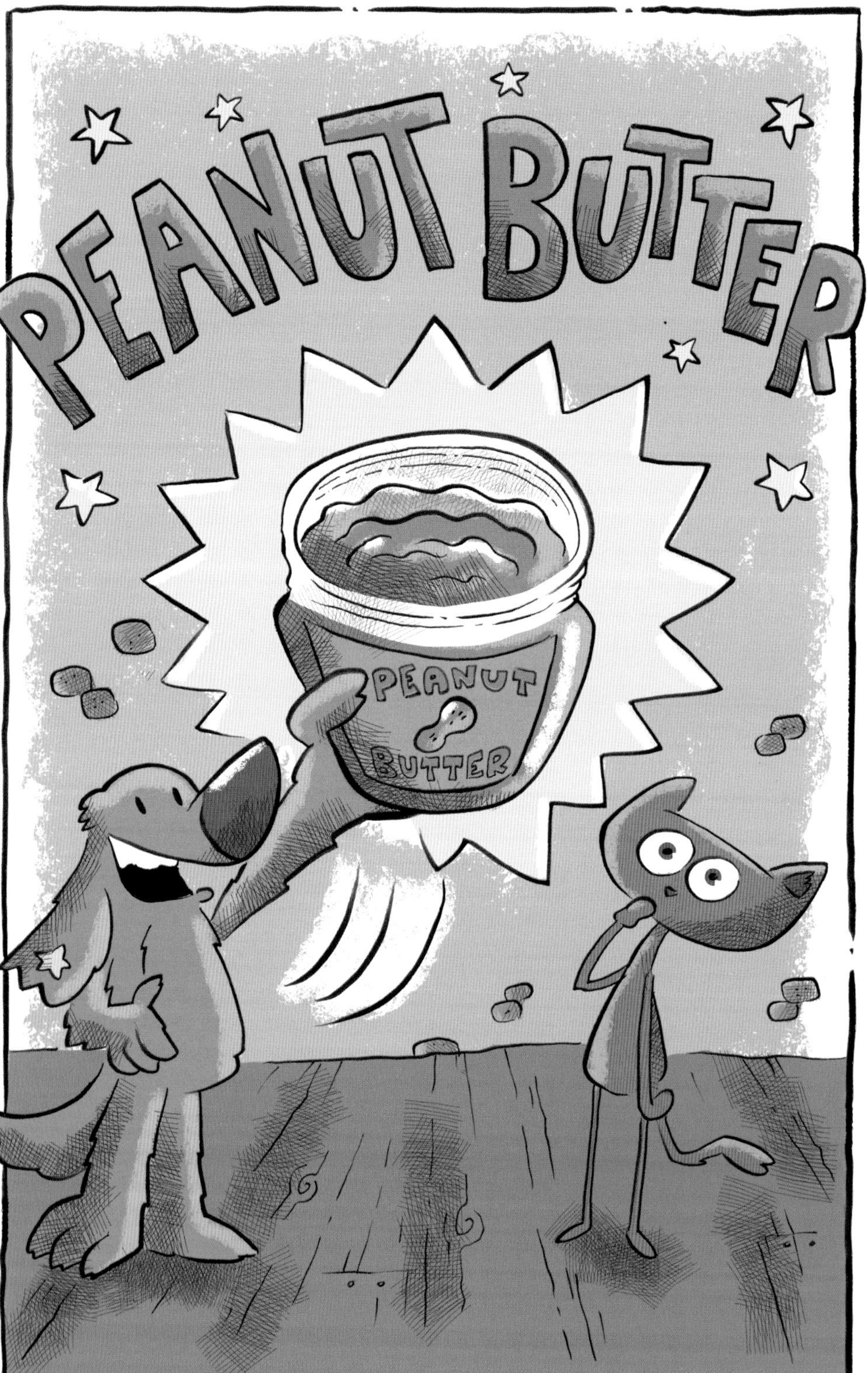
PEANUT BUTTER
PEANUT BUTTER

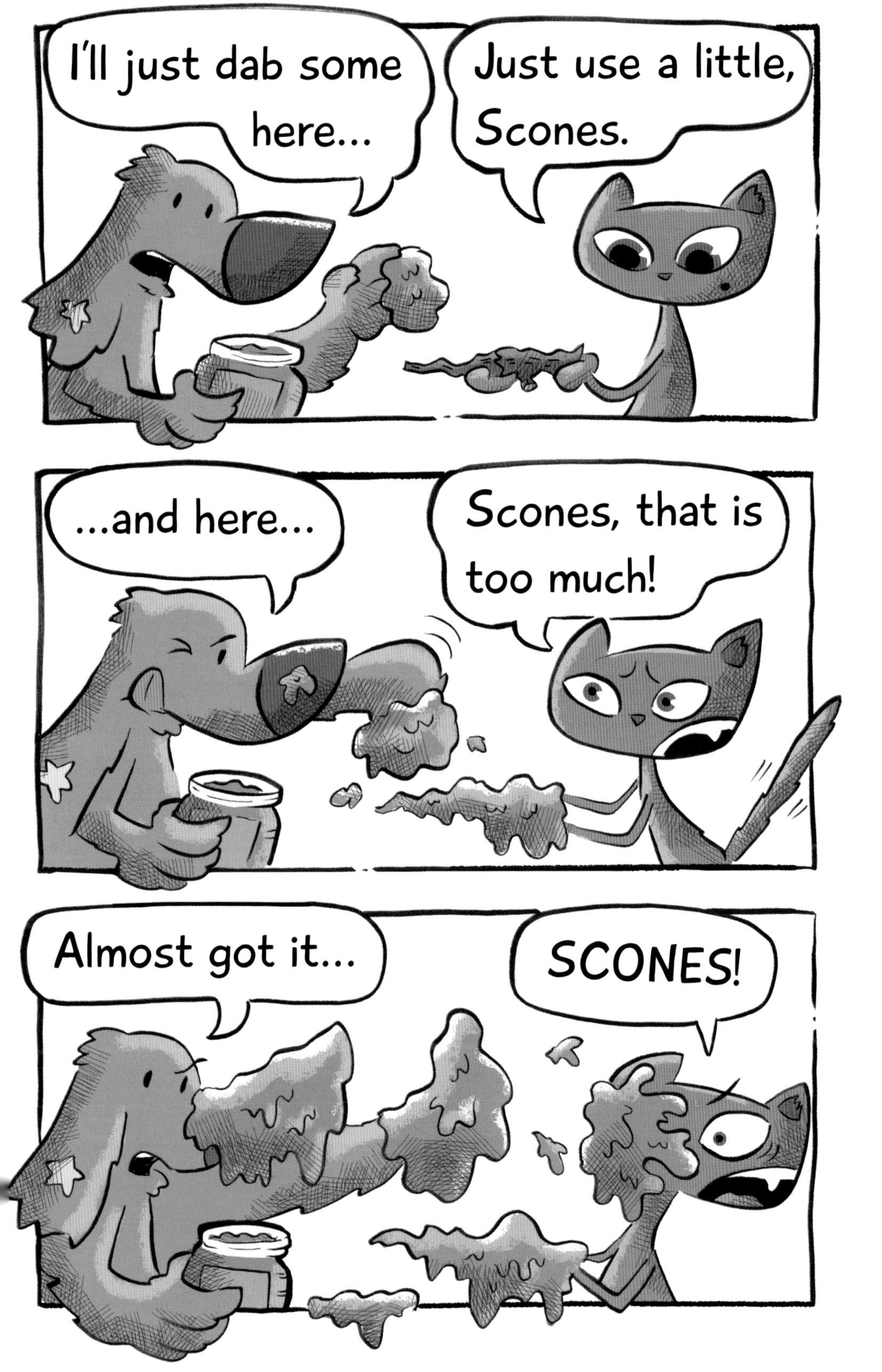
I'll just dab some here...
Just use a little, Scones.
...and here...
Scones, that is too much!
Almost got it...
SCONES!

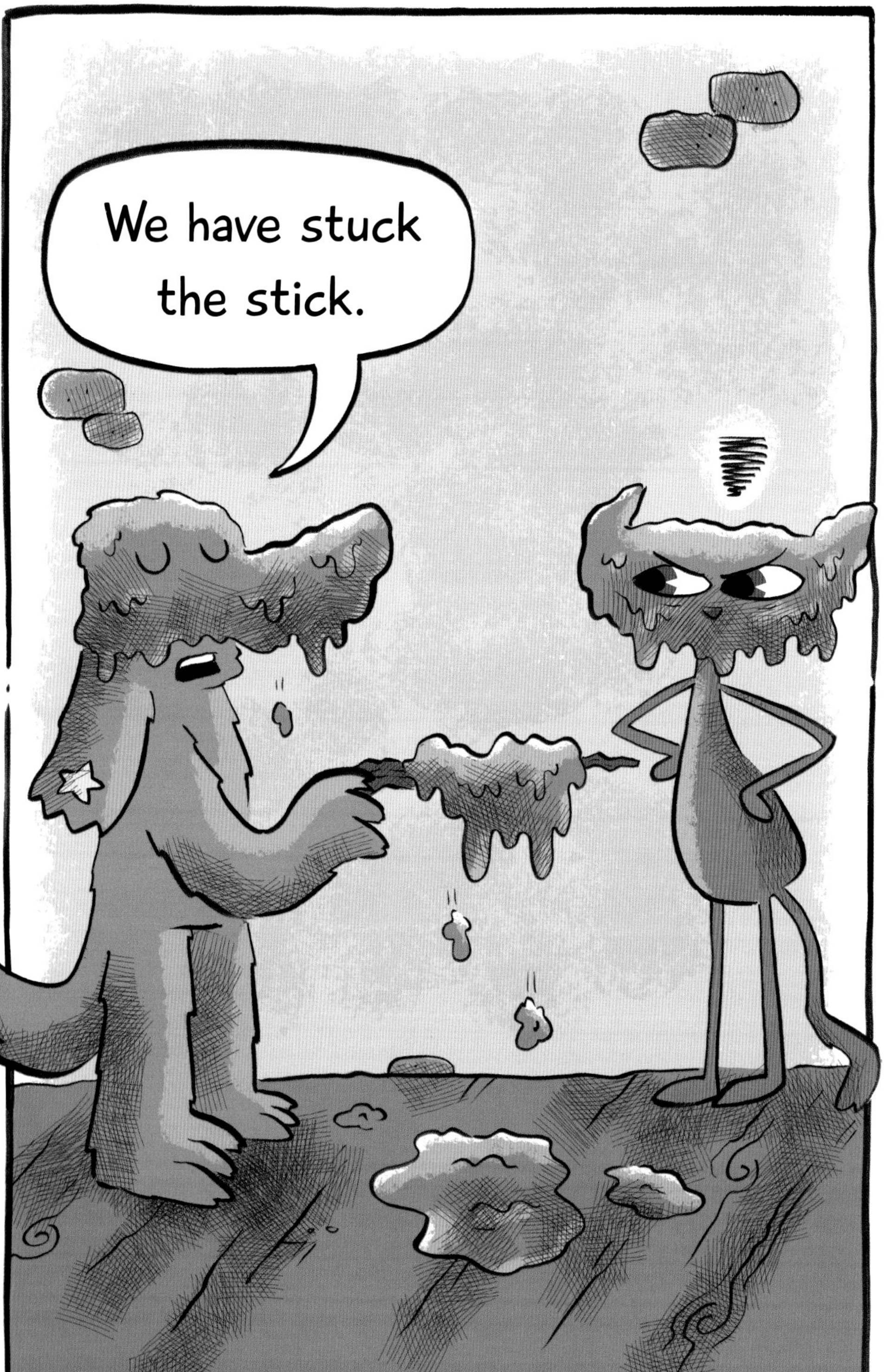
We have stuck the stick.

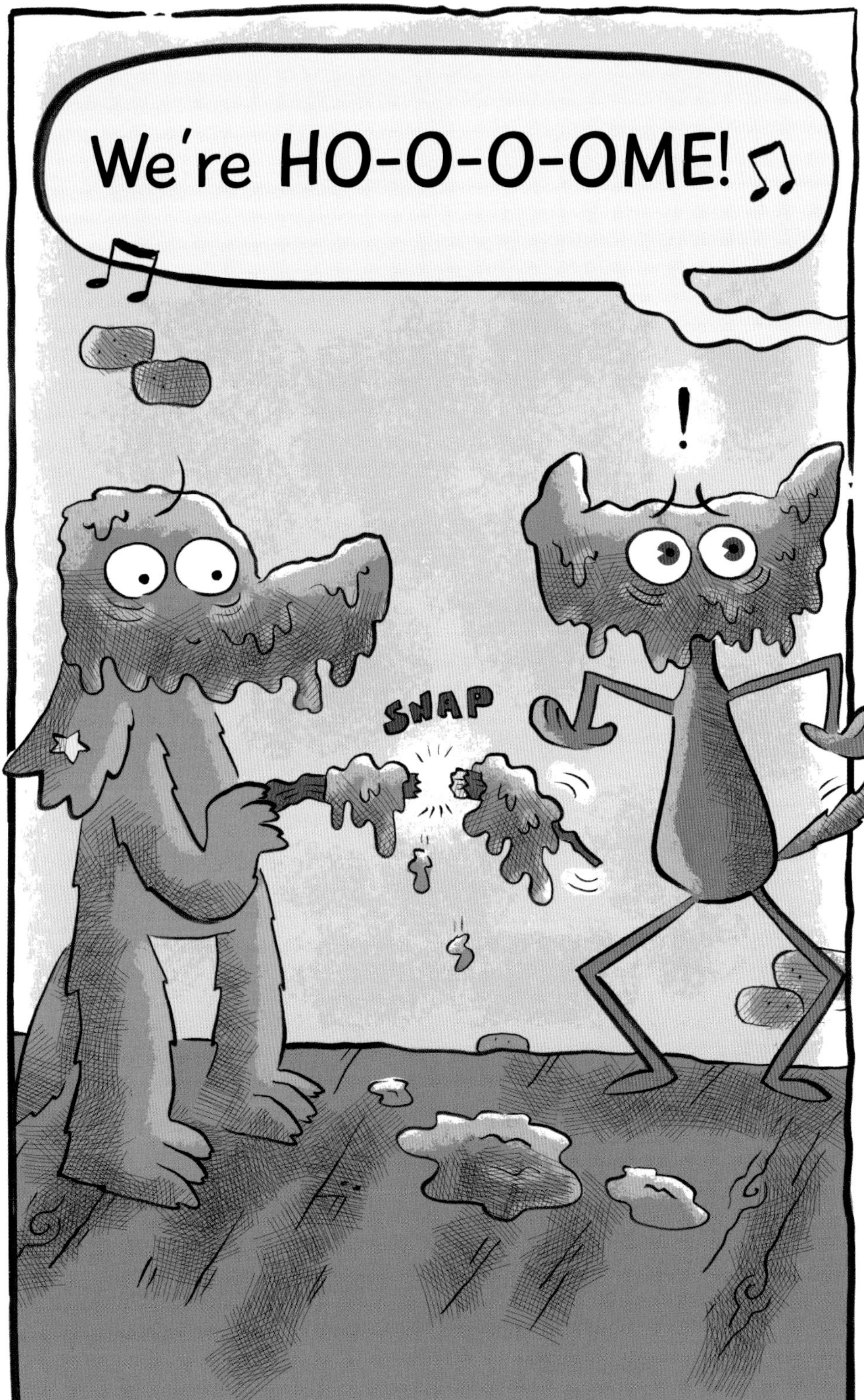
We're HO-O-O-OME!
SNAP

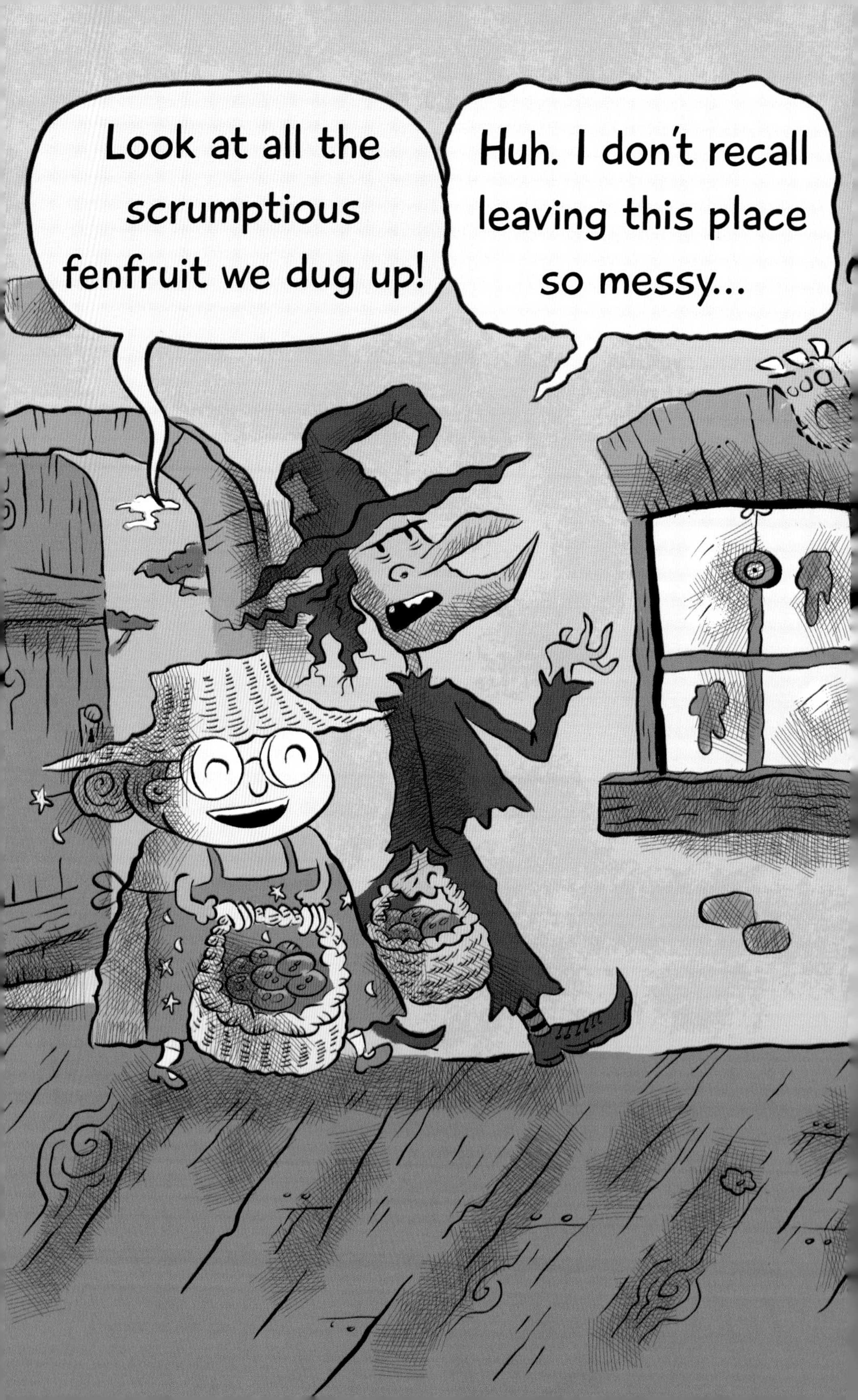
Look at all the scrumptious fenfruit we dug up!
Huh. I don't recall leaving this place so messy...

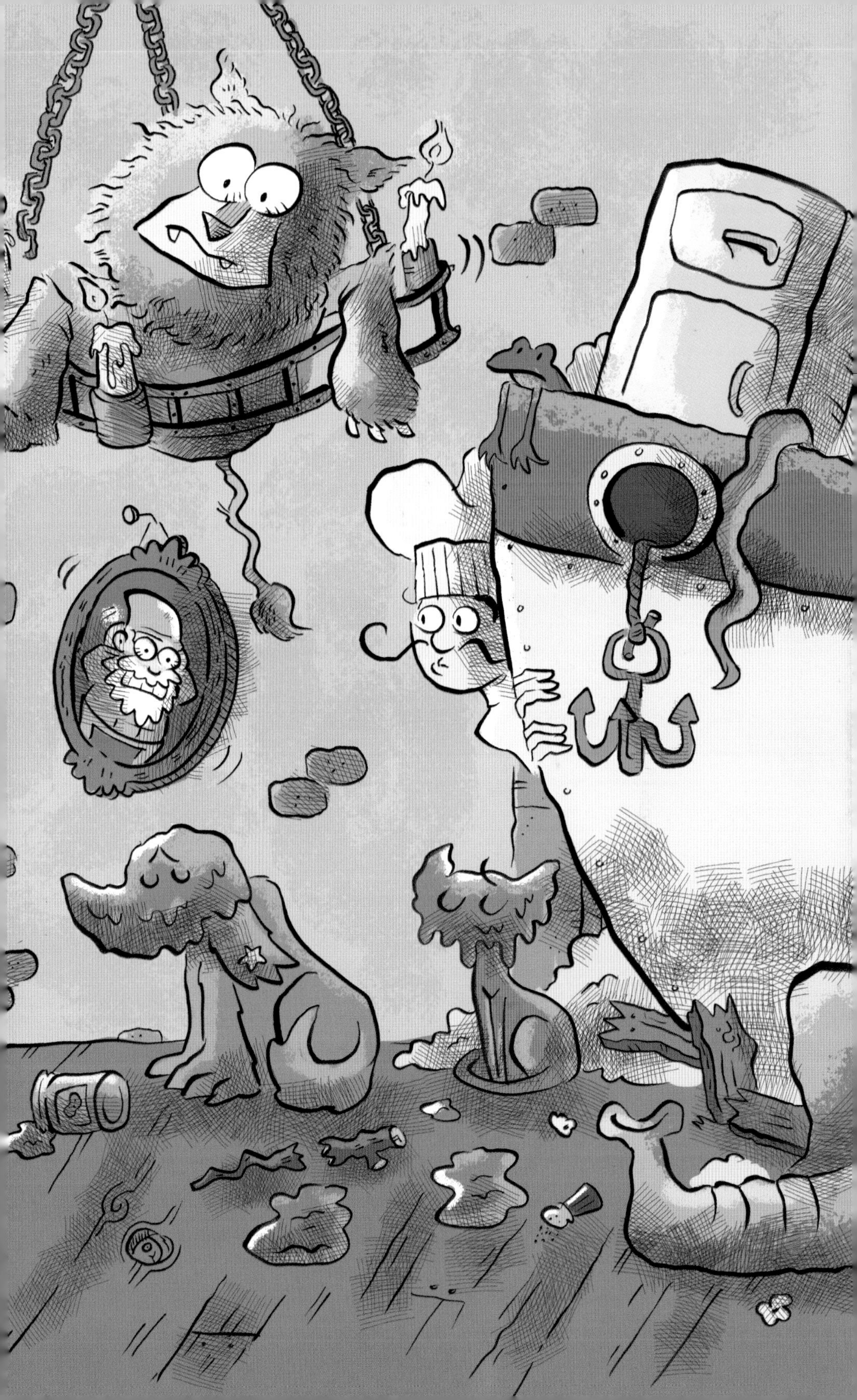

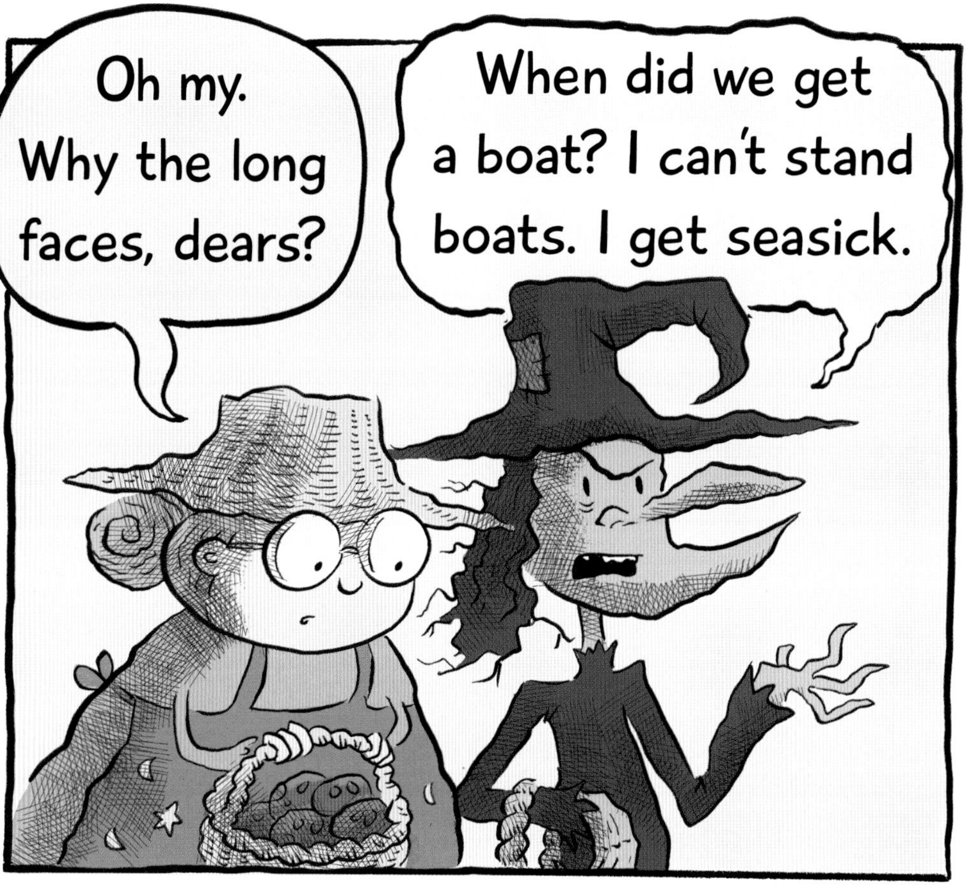
Oh my. Why the long faces, dears?
When did we get a boat? I can't stand boats. I get seasick.

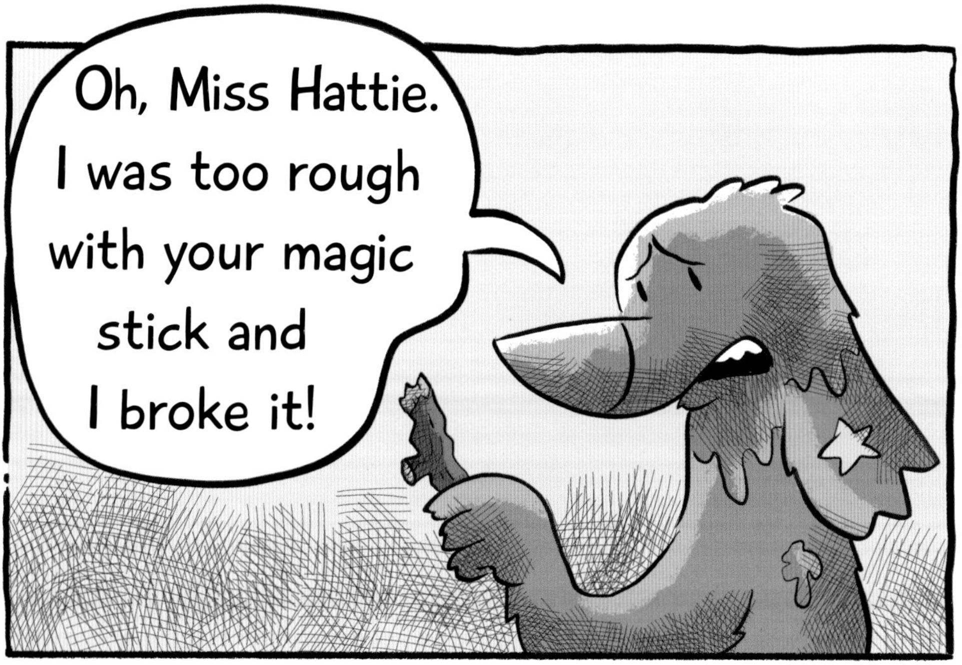
Oh, Miss Hattie. I was too rough with your magic stick and I broke it!

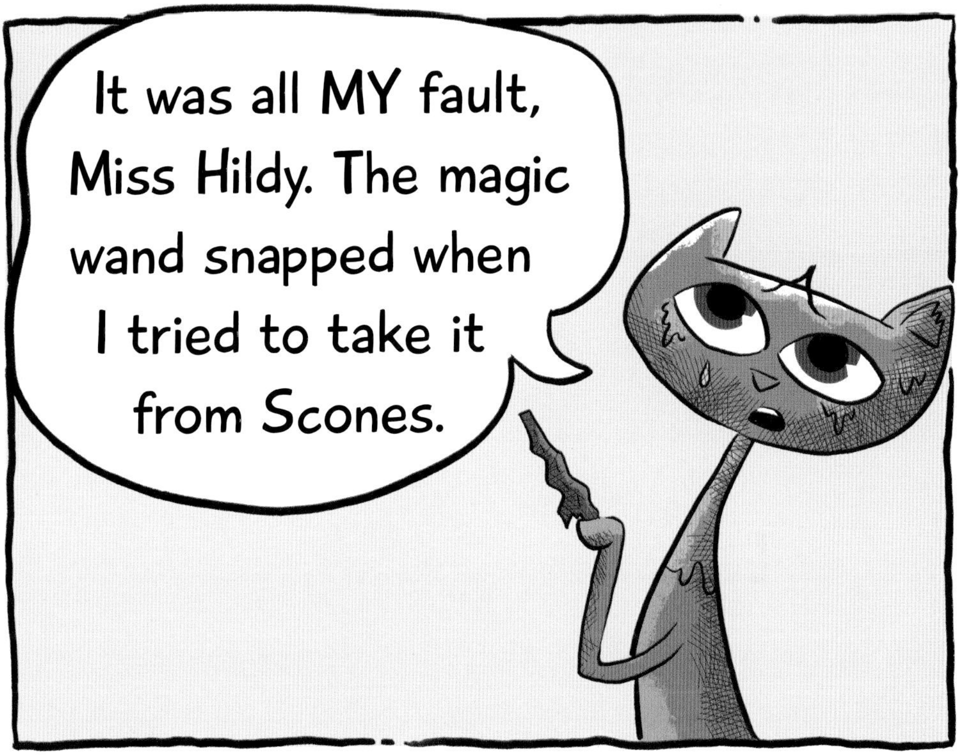
It was all MY fault, Miss Hildy. The magic wand snapped when I tried to take it from Scones.

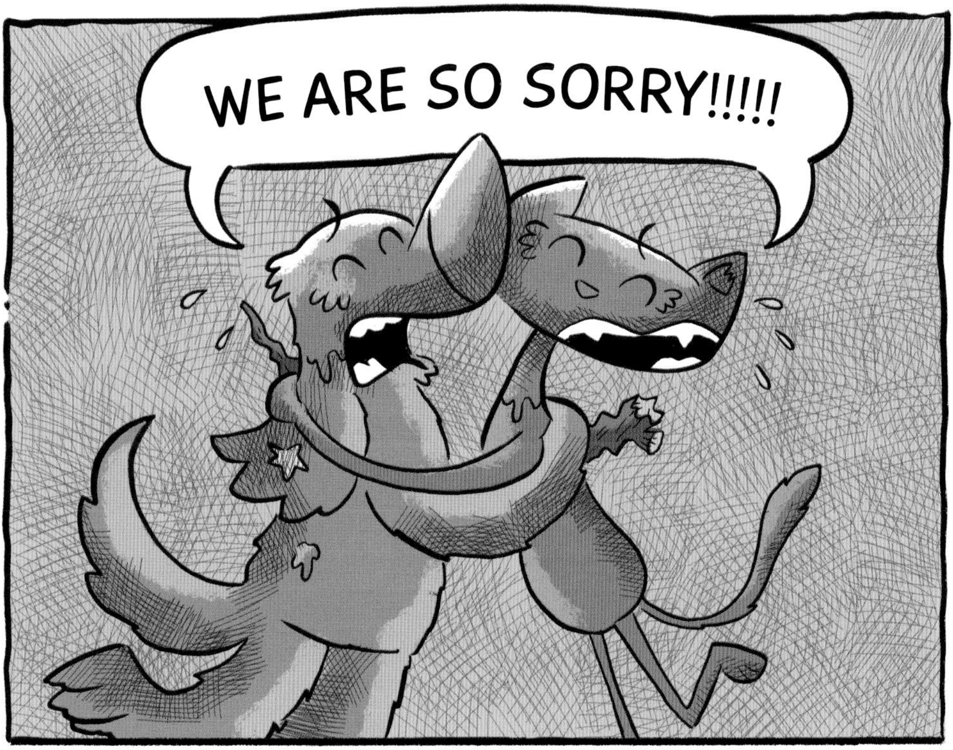
WE ARE SO SORRY!!!!!

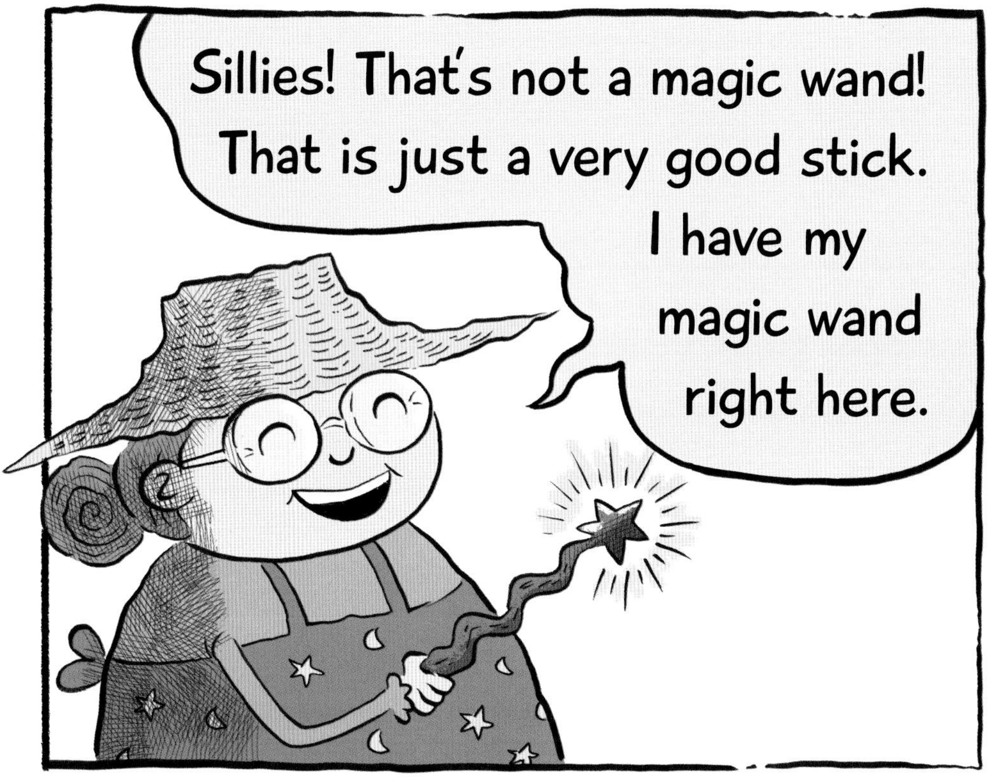
Sillies! That's not a magic wand! That is just a very good stick.
I have my magic wand right here.

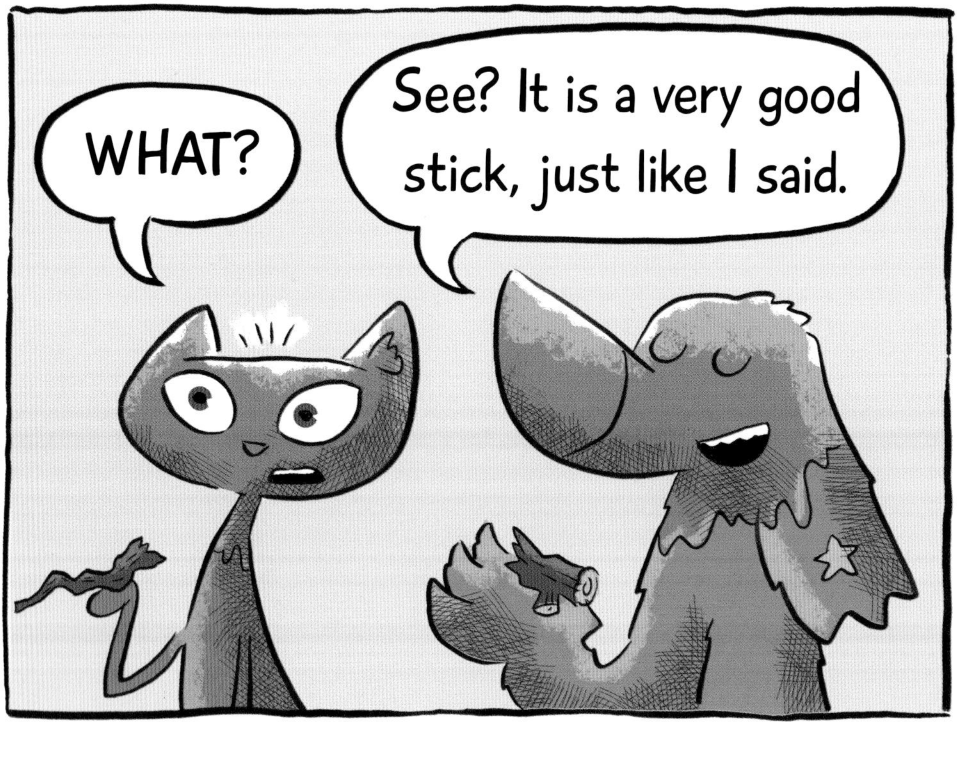
WHAT?
See? It is a very good stick, just like I said.

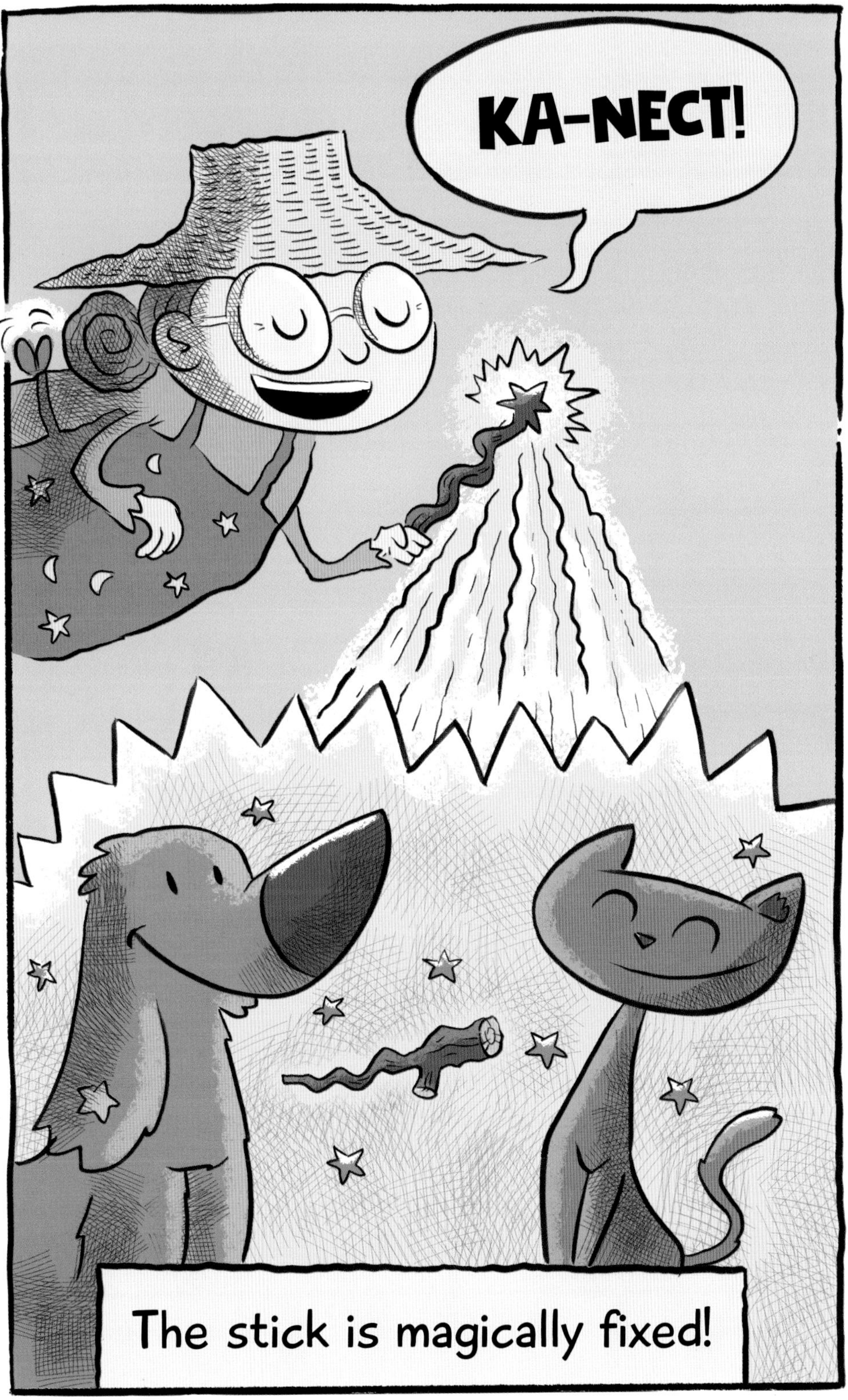
KA-NECT!
The stick is magically fixed!

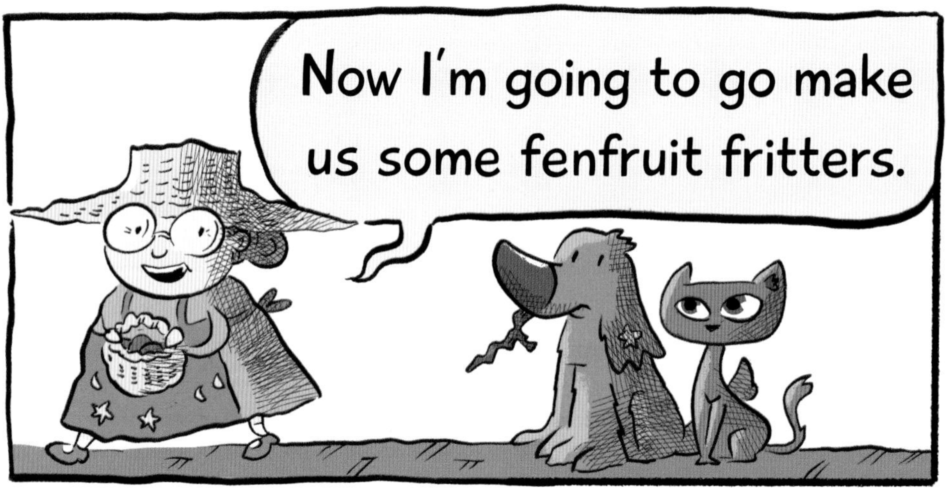
Now I'm going to go make us some fenfruit fritters.

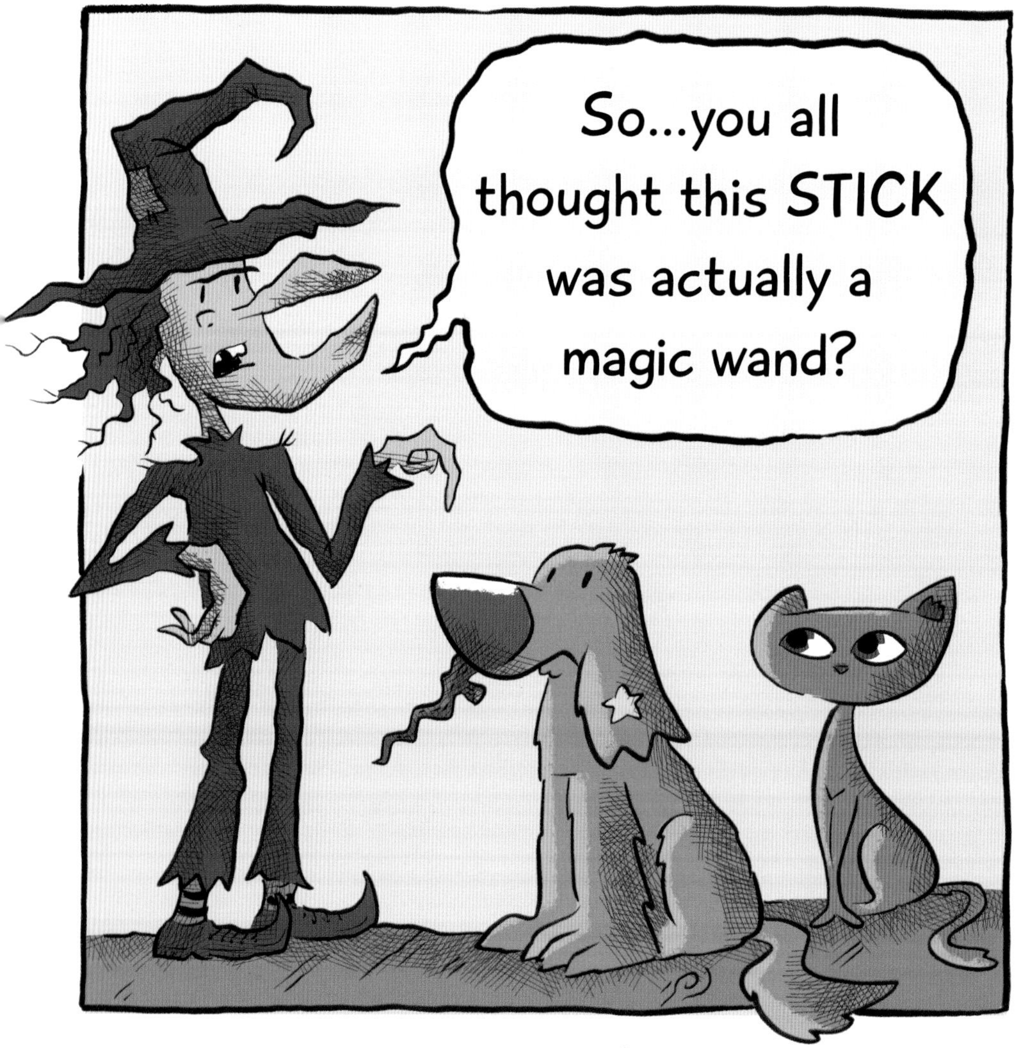
So...you all thought this STICK was actually a magic wand?

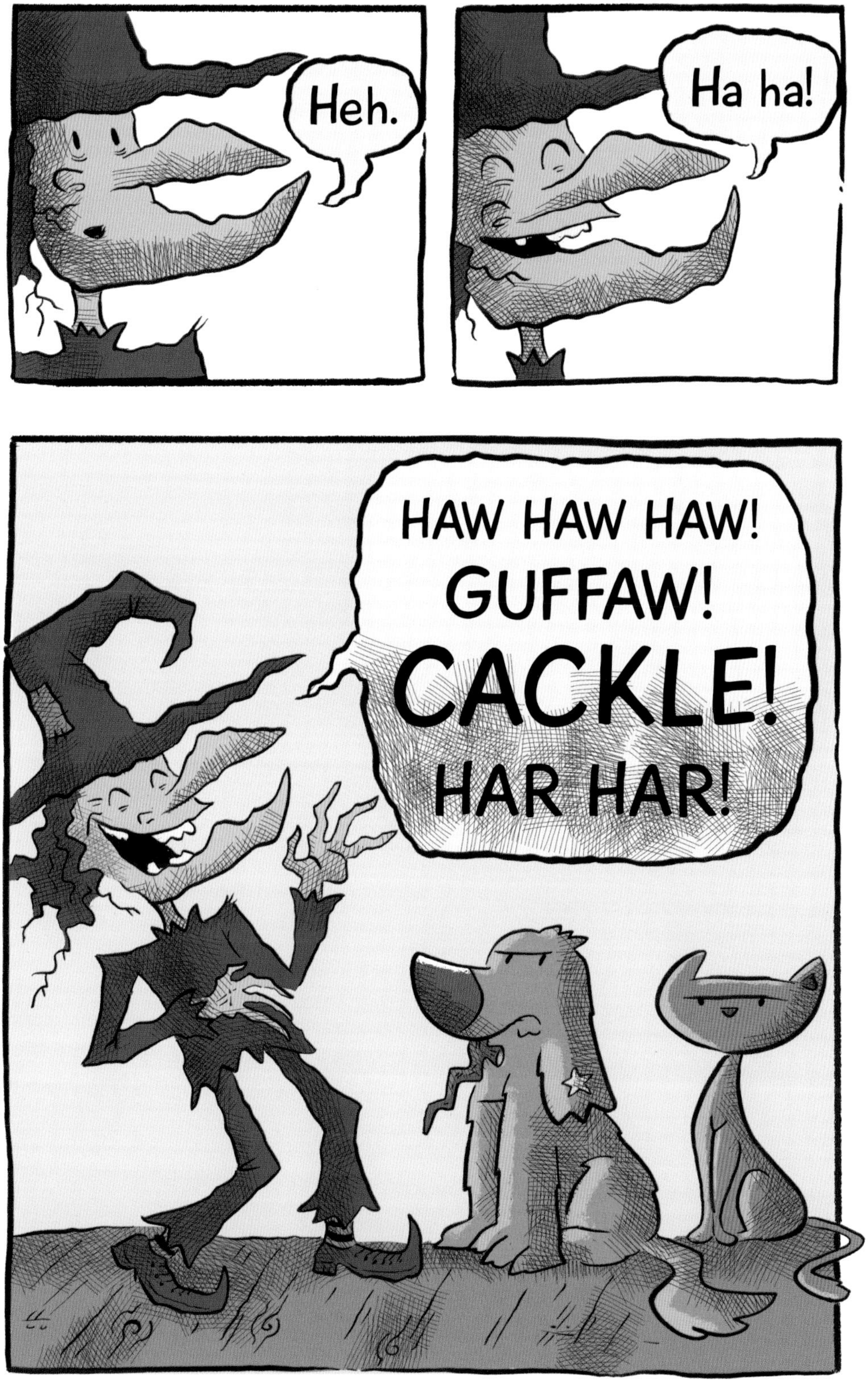
Heh.
Ha ha!
HAW HAW HAW! GUFFAW! CACKLE! HAR HAR!

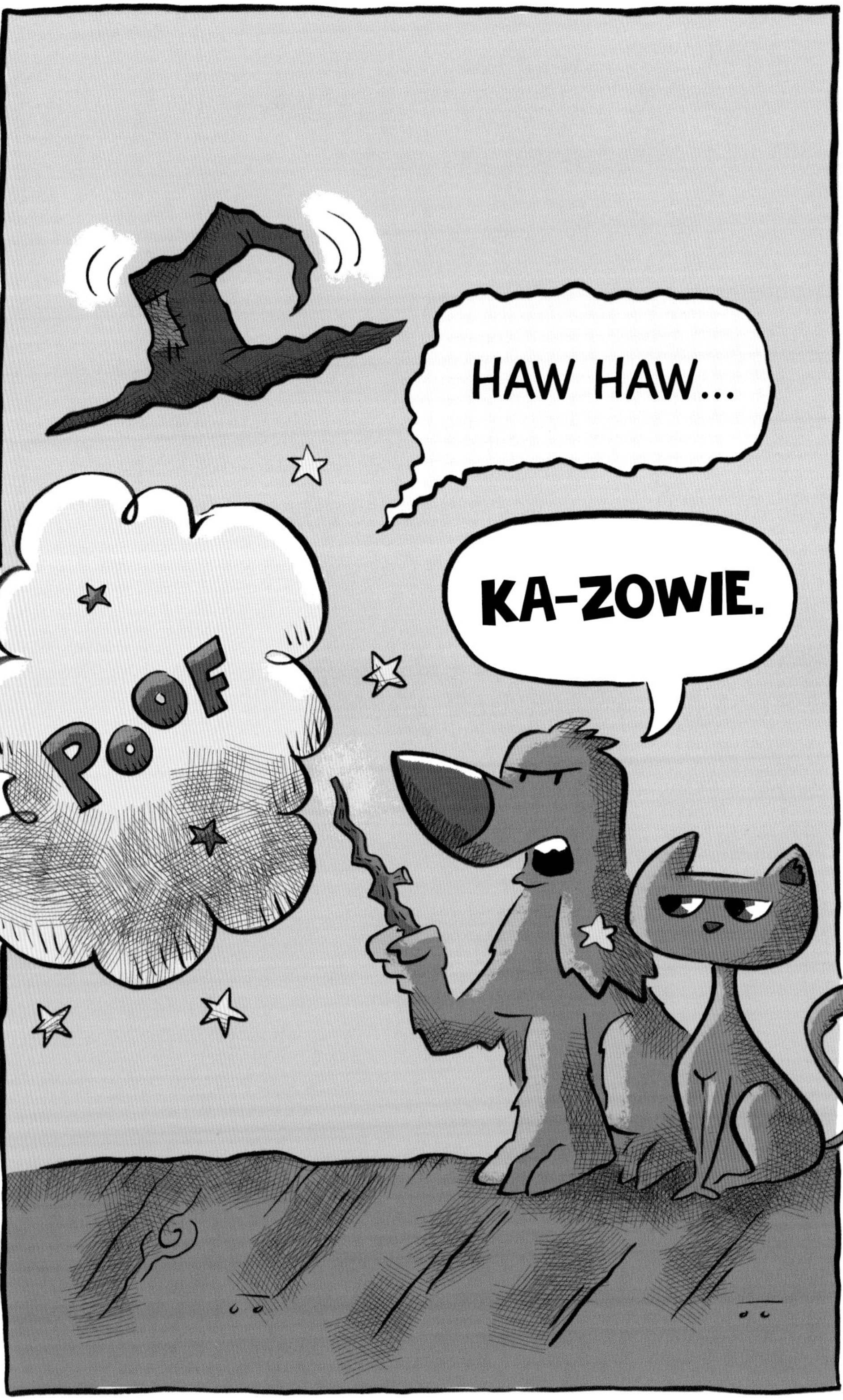
HAW HAW...
KA-ZOWIE.
POOF

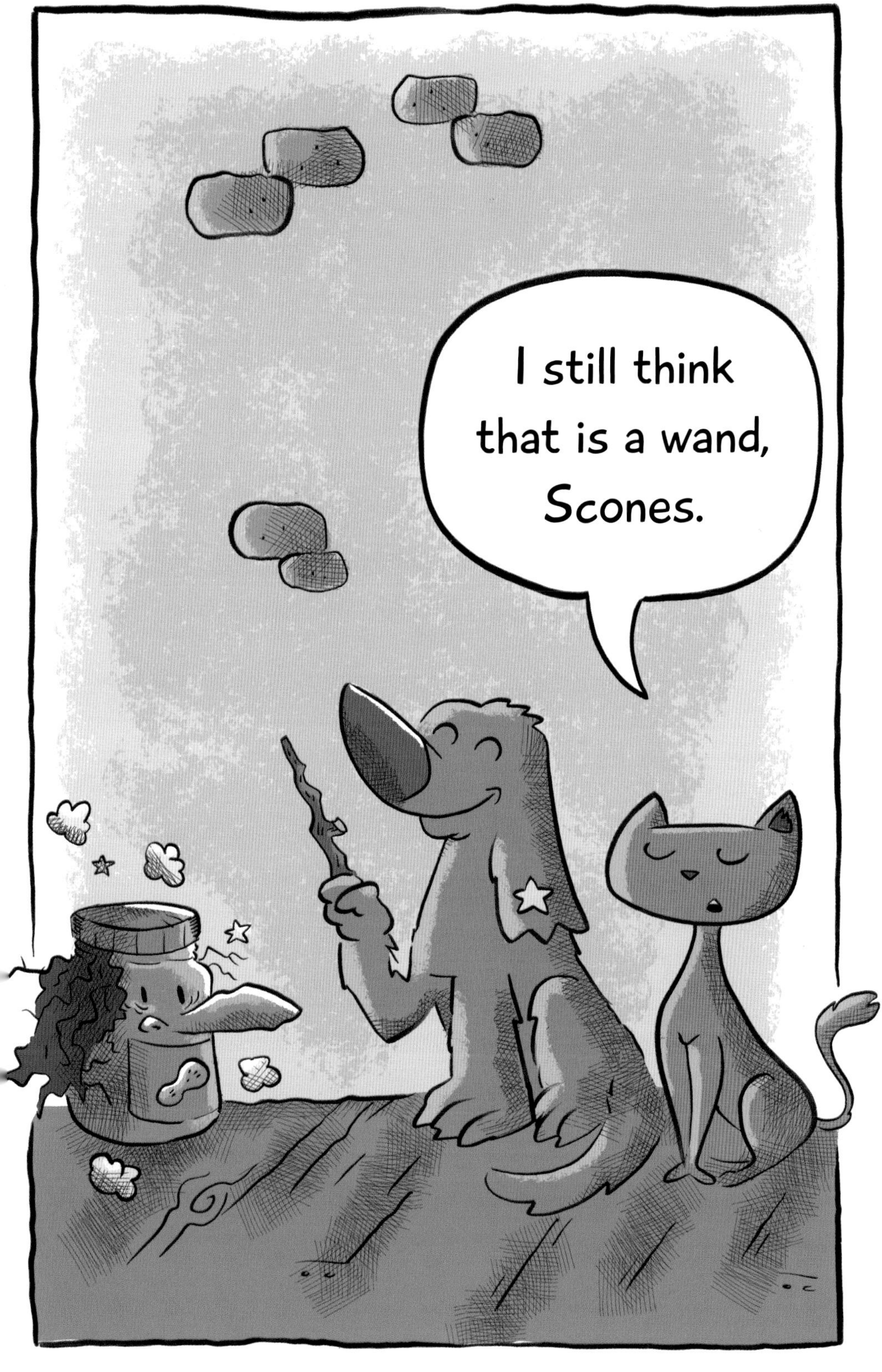
I still think that is a wand, Scones.

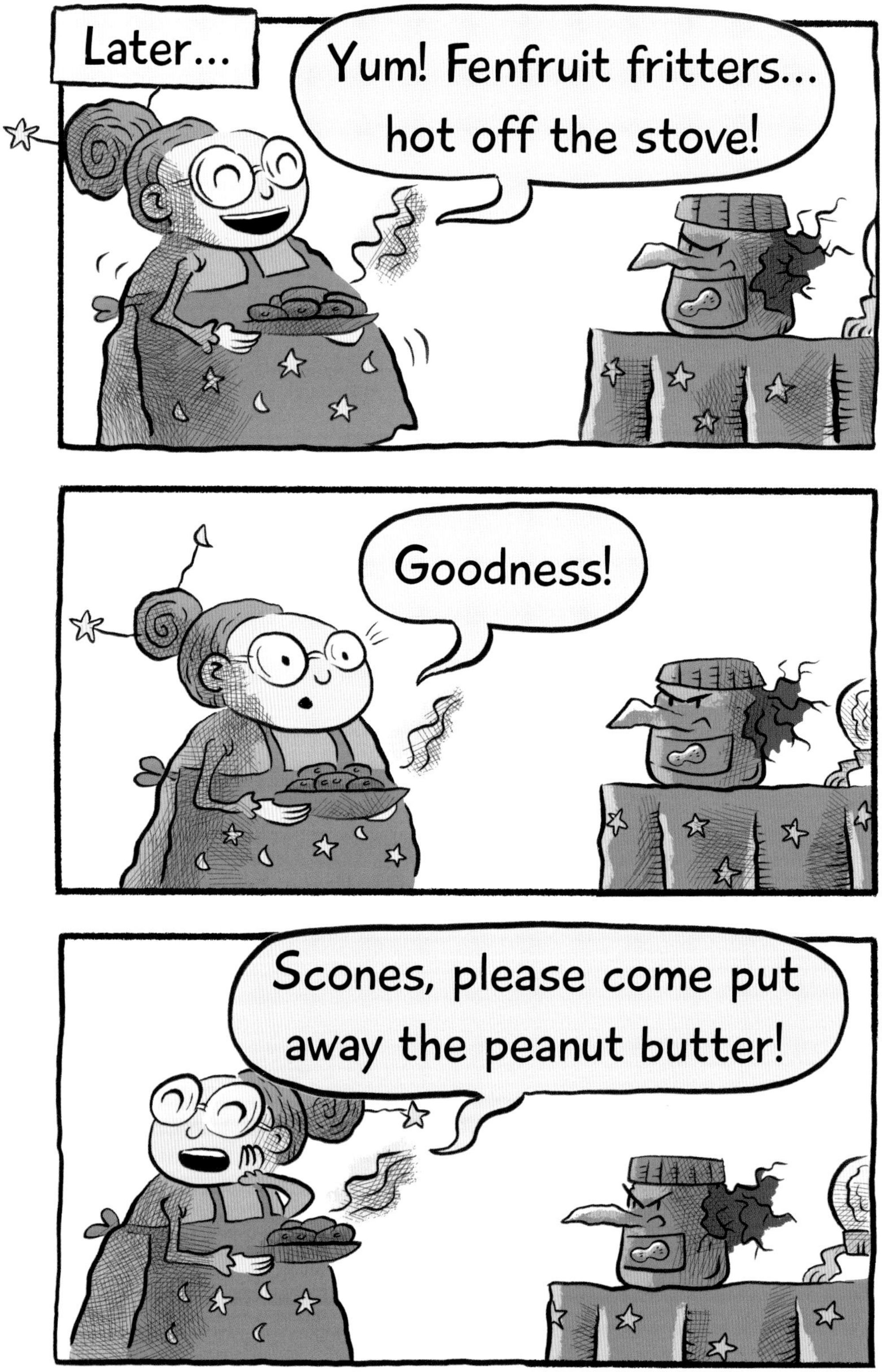
Later...
Yum! Fenfruit fritters... hot off the stove!
Goodness!
Scones, please come put away the peanut butter!

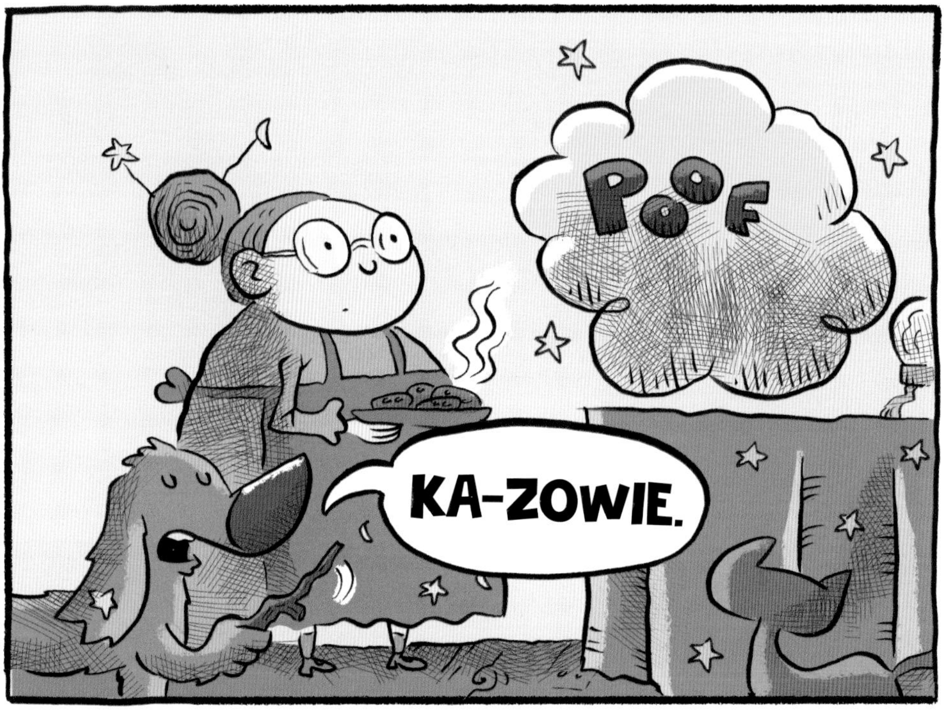
POOF
KA-ZOWIE.

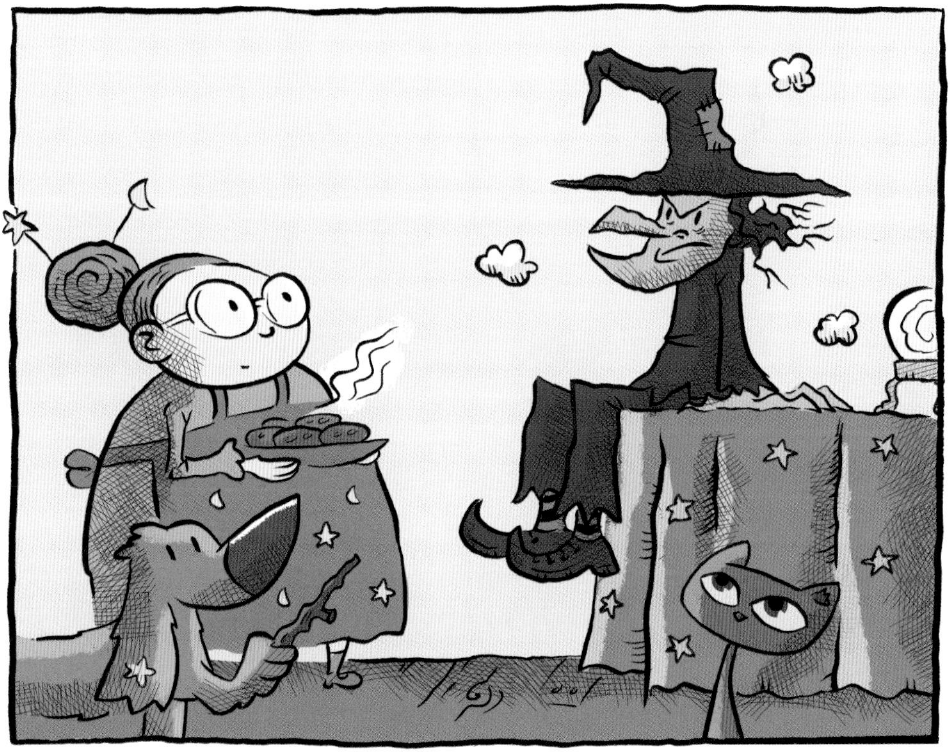

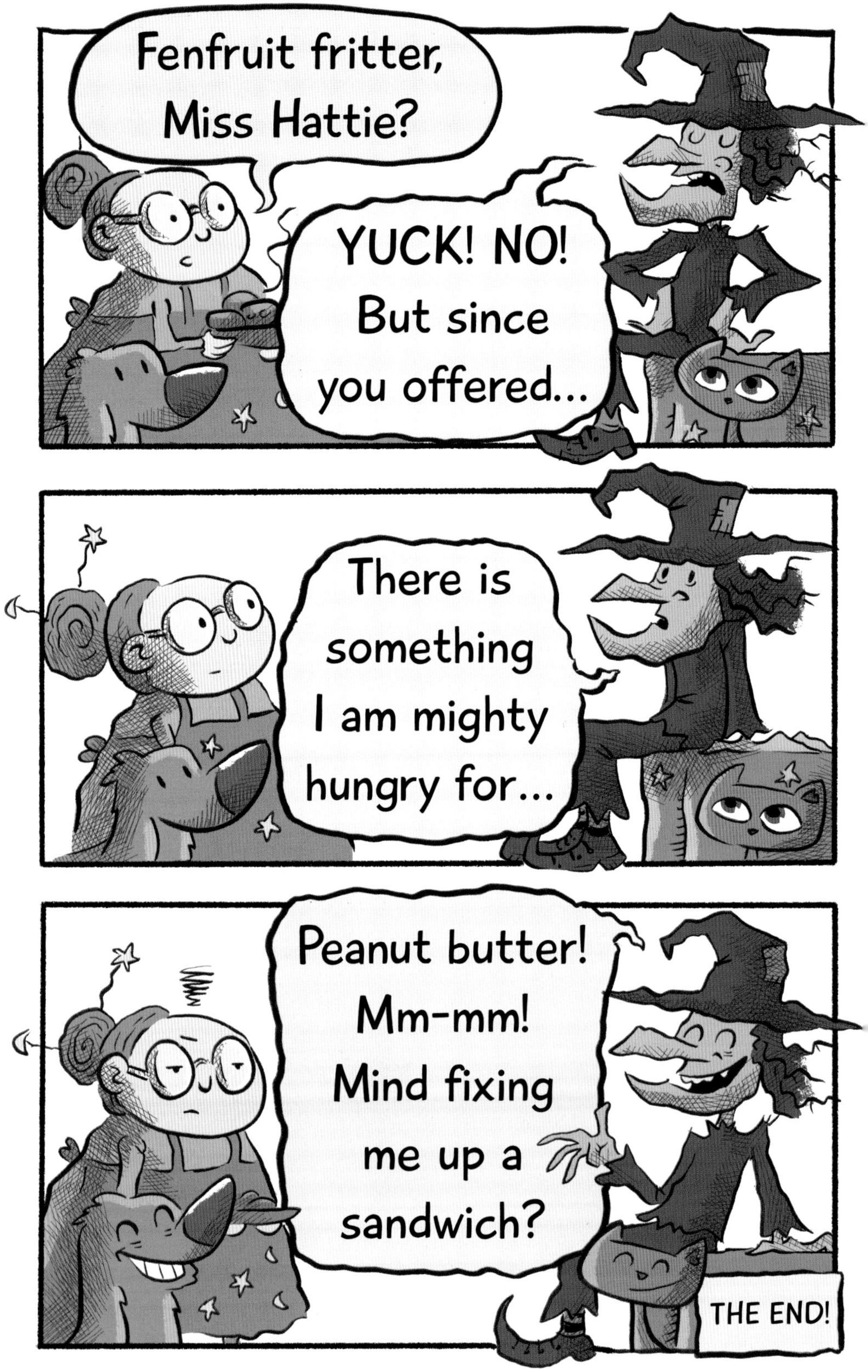

Fenfruit fritter, Miss Hattie?
YUCK! NO! But since you offered...
There is something I am mighty hungry for...
Peanut butter! Mm-mm! Mind fixing me up a sandwich?
THE END!